Colson Whitehead is the *Sunday Times* bestselling author of *The Underground Railroad*, *The Noble Hustle*, *Zone One*, *Sag Harbor*, *The Intuitionist*, *John Henry Days*, *Apex Hides the Hurt* and one collection of essays, *The Colossus of New York*. A Pulitzer Prize winner and a recipient of MacArthur and Guggenheim fellowships, he lives in New York City.

Praise for *The Nickel Boys*

'A commanding triumph . . . the prose is so loaded with quicksilver wit, it holds you in its thrall. It is a novel that not only succeeds in character, plot and moral argument but lends grace to lives all too easily shattered'

Johanna Thomas-Corr, *Sunday Times*, Books of the Year

'Forceful and tightly wrought . . . Whitehead homes in on the way in which every action fits into a fully orchestrated whole, which is why I would wish everyone, black or white, to read this novel. He demonstrates to superb effect how racism in America has long operated as a codified and sanctioned activity intended to enrich one group at the expense of another'

Aminatta Forna, *Guardian*

'From the award-winning author of *The Underground Railroad* comes another searing novel exploring America's racially troubled past . . . a real page-turner'

Max Davidson, *Mail on Sunday*

'Whitehead has produced yet another modern classic . . . Quietly and purposefully heart-breaking in its portrayal of the lifelong legacy of abuse, it is quite outstanding'

Cross, *Daily Mail*

'If greatness is excellence sustained over time, then without question, Whitehead is one of the greatest of his generation. In fact, figuring his age, acclaim, productivity and consistency, he is one of the greatest American writers alive'

Mitchell S. Jackson, *Time*

'A story of courage, cruelty and perversion, set in a Southern reform school in the early 1960s. Not comfortable reading, but compelling'

Allan Massie, *Scotsman*

'There's hardly a spare word in this book ... Whitehead has a talent for creating ambiguous, complex scenes that fix in your memory. *The Nickel Boys* feels like a necessary fictional project, writing the blank or buried pages of US history; and it's done with virtuosity'

Jerome Boyd Maunsell, *Evening Standard*

'A tense, nervy performance, even more rigorously controlled than its predecessor. The narration is disciplined and the sentences plain and sturdy, oars cutting into the water. Every chapter hits its mark'

Parul Sehgal, *New York Times*

'Whitehead lays bare the brutality of recent US history and the legacy its victims carry to the bitter end'

Financial Times, Books of the Year

'*The Nickel Boys* is in conversation with works by James Baldwin, Ralph Ellison and especially Martin Luther King ... It shreds our easy confidence in the triumph of goodness and leaves in its place a hard and bitter truth about the ongoing American experiment'

Ron Charles, *Washington Post*

'What elevates Whitehead's treatment of race and American brutality is the elegance of its style and the satisfying inventiveness of its form'

Philip Hensher, *Spectator*, Books of the Year

'A haunting tale'

Tom Gatti, *New Statesman*, Books of the Year

'*The Nickel Boys* lifts the lid on the racist brutality of reform schools in the Jim Crow-era south'

Justine Jordan, *Guardian*

'Whitehead's most emotionally resonant novel to date ... he allows us to feel, and to ache, too'

Clifford Thompson, *Times Literary Supplement*

'A furious, compassionate novel whose final sleight of hand will twist deep in your gut'

Claire Allfree, *Metro*

'Haunting and haunted ... The book feels like a mission, and it's an essential one'

Frank Rich, *New York Times Book Review*

'Searing ... the story is masterfully told'

Duncan White, *Telegraph*

ALSO BY COLSON WHITEHEAD

The Intuitionist
John Henry Days
The Colossus of New York
Apex Hides the Hurt
Sag Harbor
Zone One
The Noble Hustle
The Underground Railroad

THE Nickel Boys

COLSON WHITEHEAD

FLEET
2020

FLEET

First published in Great Britain in 2019 by Fleet
This paperback edition published in 2020 by Fleet

3 5 7 9 10 8 6 4

Copyright © 2019 by Colson Whitehead

The moral right of the author has been asserted.

All characters and events in this publication, other than those clearly in the public domain, are fictitious and any resemblance to real persons, living or dead, is purely coincidental.

All rights reserved.
No part of this publication may be reproduced, stored in a retrieval system, or transmitted, in any form or by any means, without the prior permission in writing of the publisher, nor be otherwise circulated in any form of binding or cover other than that in which it is published and without a similar condition including this condition being imposed on the subsequent purchaser.

A CIP catalogue record for this book
is available from the British Library.

ISBN 978-0-7088-9942-7

Book design by Pei Loi Koay
Printed and bound in Great Britain by Clays Ltd, Elcograf S.p.A.

Papers used by Fleet are from well-managed forests
and other responsible sources.

Fleet
An imprint of
Little, Brown Book Group
Carmelite House
50 Victoria Embankment
London EC4Y 0DZ

An Hachette UK Company
www.hachette.co.uk

www.littlebrown.co.uk

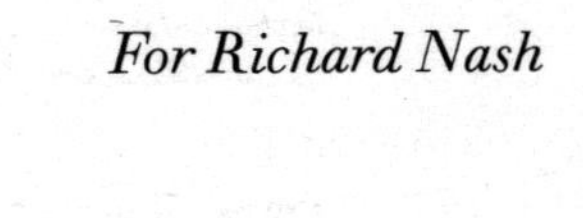

For Richard Nash

THE Nickel Boys

PROLOGUE

Even in death the boys were trouble.

The secret graveyard lay on the north side of the Nickel campus, in a patchy acre of wild grass between the old work barn and the school dump. The field had been a grazing pasture when the school operated a dairy, selling milk to local customers—one of the state of Florida's schemes to relieve the taxpayer burden of the boys' upkeep. The developers of the office park had earmarked the field for a lunch plaza, with four water features and a concrete bandstand for the occasional event. The discovery of the bodies was an expensive complication for the real estate company awaiting the all clear from the environmental study, and for the state's attorney, which had recently closed an investigation into the abuse stories. Now they had to start a new inquiry, establish the identities of the deceased and the manner of death, and there was no telling when the whole damned place could be razed, cleared, and neatly erased from history, which everyone agreed was long overdue.

All the boys knew about that rotten spot. It took a student from the University of South Florida to bring it to the rest of the world, decades after the first boy was tied up in a potato sack and dumped there. When asked how she spotted the graves, Jody said, "The dirt looked wrong." The sunken earth, the scrabbly weeds. Jody and the rest of the archaeology students from the university had been excavating the school's official cemetery for months. The state couldn't dispose of the property until the remains were properly resettled, and the archaeology students needed field credits. With stakes and wire they divided the area into search grids, dug with hand shovels and heavy equipment. After sifting the soil, bones and belt buckles and soda bottles lay scattered on their trays in an inscrutable exhibit.

The Nickel Boys called the official cemetery Boot Hill, from the Saturday matinees they had enjoyed before they were sent to the school and exiled from such pastimes. The name stuck, generations later, with the South Florida students who'd never seen a Western in their lives. Boot Hill was just over the big slope on the north campus. The white concrete *X*'s that marked the graves caught the sunlight on bright afternoons. Names were carved into two-thirds of the crosses; the rest were blank. Identification was difficult, but competition between the young archaeologists made for constant progress. The school records, though incomplete and haphazard, narrowed down who WILLIE 1954 had been. The burned remains accounted for those who perished in the dormitory fire of 1921. DNA matches with surviving family members—the ones the university students were able to track down—reconnected the dead to the living world that proceeded without them. Of the forty-three bodies, seven remained unnamed.

The students piled the white concrete crosses in a mound next to the excavation site. When they returned to work one morning, someone had smashed them into chunks and dust.

Boot Hill released its boys one by one. Jody was excited when she hosed down some artifacts from one of the trenches and came across her first remains. Professor Carmine told her that the little flute of bone in her hand most likely belonged to a raccoon or other small animal. The secret graveyard redeemed her. Jody found it while wandering the grounds in search of a cell signal. Her professor backed up her hunch, on account of the irregularities at the Boot Hill site: all those fractures and cratered skulls, the rib cages riddled with buckshot. If the remains from the official cemetery were suspicious, what had befallen those in the unmarked burial ground? Two days later cadaver-sniffing dogs and radar imaging confirmed matters. No white crosses, no names. Just bones waiting for someone to find them.

"They called this a school," Professor Carmine said. You can hide a lot in an acre, in the dirt.

One of the boys or one of their relatives tipped off the media. The students had a relationship with some of the boys at that point, after all the interviews. The boys reminded them of crotchety uncles and flinty characters from their old neighborhoods, men who might soften once you got to know them but never lost that hard center. The archaeology students told the boys about the second burial site, told the family members of the dead kids they'd dug up, and then a local Tallahassee station dispatched a reporter. Plenty of boys had talked of the secret graveyard before, but as it had ever been with Nickel, no one believed them until someone else said it.

The national press picked up the story and people got their first real look at the reform school. Nickel had been closed for three years, which explained the savagery of the grounds and the standard teenage vandalism. Even the most innocent scene—a mess hall or the football field—came out sinister, no photographic trickery necessary. The footage was unsettling. Shadows crept and trembled at the corners and each stain or mark looked like dried blood. As if every image caught by the video rig emerged with its dark nature exposed, the Nickel you could see going in and then the Nickel you couldn't see coming out.

If that happened to the harmless places, what do you think the haunted places looked like?

Nickel Boys were cheaper than a dime-a-dance and you got more for your money, or so they used to say. In recent years, some of the former students organized support groups, reuniting over the internet and meeting in diners and McDonald's. Around someone's kitchen table after an hour's drive. Together they performed their own phantom archaeology, digging through decades and restoring to human eyes the shards and artifacts of those days. Each man with his own pieces. *He used to say, I'll pay you a visit later. The wobbly stairs to the schoolhouse basement. The blood squished between my toes in my tennis shoes.* Reassembling those fragments into confirmation of a shared darkness: If it is true for you, it is true for someone else, and you are no longer alone.

Big John Hardy, a retired carpet salesman from Omaha, maintained a website for the Nickel Boys with the latest news. He kept the others apprised on the petition for another investigation and how the statement of apology from the government was coming along. A blinking digital widget kept track of the fund-raising for the proposed memorial. E-mail Big John the story of your Nickel days and he'd post it with your picture. Sharing a link with your family was a way of saying, This is where I was made. An explanation and an apology.

The annual reunion, now in its fifth year, was strange and necessary. The boys were old men now, with wives and ex-wives and children they did or didn't talk to, with wary grandchildren who were brought around sometimes and those whom they were prevented from seeing. They had managed to scrape up a life after leaving Nickel or had never fit in at all with normal people. The last smokers of cigarette brands you never see, late to the self-help regimens, always on the verge of disappearing. Dead in prison, or decomposing in rooms they rented by the week, frozen to death in the woods after drinking turpentine. The men met in the conference room of the Eleanor Garden Inn to catch up before caravaning out to Nickel for the solemn tour. Some years you felt strong enough to head down that concrete walkway, knowing that it led to one of your bad places, and some years you didn't. Avoid a building or stare it in the face, depending on your reserves that morning. Big John posted a report after each reunion for those who couldn't make it.

In New York City there lived a Nickel Boy who went by the name of Elwood Curtis. He'd do a web search on the old reform school now and then, see if there were any developments, but he stayed away from the reunions and didn't add his name to the lists, for many reasons. What was the point? Grown men. What, you take turns handing each other Kleenex? One of the others posted a story about the night he parked outside Spencer's house, watching the windows for hours, the silhouette figures inside, until he talked himself out of revenge. He'd made his own leather strap to use on the superintendent. Elwood didn't get it. Go all that way, might as well follow through.

When they found the secret graveyard, he knew he'd have to return. The clutch of cedars over the TV reporter's shoulder brought back the heat on his skin, the screech of the dry flies. It wasn't far off at all. Never will be.

PART One

CHAPTER ONE

Elwood received the best gift of his life on Christmas Day 1962, even if the ideas it put in his head were his undoing. *Martin Luther King at Zion Hill* was the only album he owned and it never left the turntable. His grandmother Harriet had a few gospel records, which she only played when the world discovered a new mean way to work on her, and Elwood wasn't allowed to listen to the Motown groups or popular songs like that on account of their licentious nature. The rest of his presents that year were clothes—a new red sweater, socks—and he certainly wore those out, but nothing endured such good and constant use as the record. Every scratch and pop it gathered over the months was a mark of his enlightenment, tracking each time he entered into a new understanding of the reverend's words. The crackle of truth.

They didn't have a TV set but Dr. King's speeches were such a vivid chronicle—containing all that the Negro had been and all that he would be—that the record was almost as good as television. Maybe even better, grander, like the towering screen at the Davis Drive-In, which he'd been to twice. Elwood saw it all: Africans persecuted by the white sin of slavery, Negroes humiliated and kept low by segregation, and that luminous image to come, when all those places closed to his race were opened.

The speeches had been recorded all over, Detroit and Charlotte and Montgomery, connecting Elwood to the rights struggle across the country. One speech even made him feel like a member of the King family. Every kid had heard of Fun Town, been there or envied someone who had. In the third cut on side A, Dr. King spoke of how his daughter longed to visit the amusement park on Stewart Avenue in Atlanta. Yolanda begged her parents whenever she spotted the big sign from the expressway or the commercials came on TV. Dr. King had to tell her in his low, sad rumble about the segregation system that kept colored boys and girls on the other side of the fence. Explain the misguided thinking of some whites—not all whites, but enough whites—that gave it force and meaning. He counseled his daughter to resist the lure of hatred and bitterness and assured her that "Even though you can't go to Fun Town, I want you to know that you are as good as anybody who goes into Fun Town."

That was Elwood—as good as anyone. Two hundred and thirty miles south of Atlanta, in Tallahassee. Sometimes he saw a Fun Town commercial while visiting his cousins in Georgia. Lurching rides and happy music, chipper white kids lining up for the Wild Mouse Roller Coaster, Dick's Mini Golf. Strap into the Atomic Rocket for a trip to the moon. A perfect report card guaranteed free admission, the commercials said, if your teacher stamped a red mark on it. Elwood got all A's and kept his stack of evidence for the day they opened Fun Town to all God's children, as Dr. King promised. "I'll get in free every day for a month, easy," he told his grandmother, lying on the front-room rug and tracing a threadbare patch with his thumb.

His grandmother Harriet had rescued the rug from the alley behind the Richmond Hotel after the last renovation. The bureau in her room, the tiny table next to Elwood's bed, and three lamps were also Richmond castoffs. Harriet had worked at the hotel since she was fourteen, when she had joined her mother on the cleaning staff. Once Elwood entered high school, the hotel manager Mr. Parker made it clear he'd hire him as a porter whenever he wanted, smart kid like him, and the white man was disappointed when the boy began working at Marconi's Tobacco & Cigars. Mr. Parker was always kind to the family, even after he had to fire Elwood's mother for stealing.

Elwood liked the Richmond and he liked Mr. Parker, but adding a fourth generation to the hotel's accounts made him uneasy in a way he found difficult to describe. Even before the encyclopedias. When he was younger, he sat on a crate in the hotel kitchen after school, reading comic books and Hardy Boys while his grandmother straightened and scrubbed upstairs. With both his parents gone, she preferred to have her nine-year-old grandson nearby instead of alone in the house. Seeing Elwood with the kitchen men made her think those afternoons were a kind of school in their own right, that it was good for him to be around men. The cooks and waiters took the boy for a mascot, playing hide-and-seek with him and peddling creaky wisdom on various topics: the white man's ways, how to treat a good-time gal, strategies for hiding money around the house. Elwood didn't understand what the older men talked about most of the time, but he nodded gamely before returning to his adventure stories.

After rushes, Elwood sometimes challenged the dishwashers to plate-drying races and they made a good-natured show of being disappointed by his superior skills. They liked seeing his smile and his odd delight at each win. Then the staff turned over. The new downtown hotels poached personnel, cooks came and went, a few of the waiters didn't return after the kitchen reopened from flood damage. With the change in staff, Elwood's races changed from endearing novelty to mean-spirited hustle; the latest dishwashers were tipped off that the grandson of one of the cleaning girls did your work for you if you told him it was a game, keep on the lookout. Who was this serious boy who loitered around while the rest of them busted their asses, getting little pats on the head from Mr. Parker like he was a damn puppy, nose in a comic book like he hadn't a care? The new men in the kitchen had different kinds of lessons to impart to a young mind. Stuff they'd learned about the world. Elwood remained unaware that the premise of the competition had changed. When he issued a challenge, everybody in the kitchen tried not to smirk.

Elwood was twelve when the encyclopedias appeared. One of the busboys dragged a stack of boxes into the kitchen and called for a powwow. Elwood squeezed in—it was a set of encyclopedias that a traveling salesman had left behind in one of the rooms upstairs. There were legends about the valuables that rich white people left in their rooms, but it was rare that this kind of plunder made it down to their domain. Barney the cook opened the top box and held up the leather-bound volume of *Fisher's Universal Encyclopedia, Aa–Be.* He handed it to Elwood, who was surprised at how heavy it was, a brick with pages edged in red. The boy flipped through, squinting at the tiny words—*Aegean, Archimedes, Argonaut*—and had a picture of himself on the front-room couch copying words he liked. Words that looked interesting on the page or that sounded interesting in his imagined pronunciations.

Cory the busboy offered up his find—he didn't know how to read and had no immediate plans to learn. Elwood made his bid. Given the personality of the kitchen, it was hard to think of anyone else who'd want the encyclopedias. Then Pete, one of the new dishwashers, said he'd race him for it.

Pete was a gawky Texan who'd started working two months prior. He was hired to bus tables, but after a few incidents they moved him to the kitchen. He looked over his shoulder when he worked, as if worried about being watched, and didn't talk much, although his gravelly laughter made the other men in the kitchen direct their jokes toward him over time. Pete wiped his hands on his pants and said, "We got time before the dinner service, if you're up for it."

The kitchen made a proper contest of it. The biggest yet. A stopwatch was produced and handed to Len, the gray-haired waiter who'd worked at the hotel for more than twenty years. He was meticulous about his black serving uniform, and maintained that he was always the best-dressed man in the dining room, putting the white patrons to shame. With his attention to detail, he'd make a dedicated referee. Two fifty-plate stacks were arranged, after a proper soaking supervised by Elwood and Pete. Two busboys acted as seconds for this duel, ready to hand over dry replacement rags when requested. A lookout stood at the kitchen door in case a manager happened by.

While not prone to bravado, Elwood had never lost a dish-drying contest in four years, and wore his confidence on his face. Pete had a concentrated air. Elwood didn't perceive the Texan as a threat, having out-dried the man in prior competitions. Pete was, in general, a good loser.

Len counted down from ten, and they began. Elwood stuck to the method he'd perfected over the years, mechanistic and gentle. He'd never let a wet plate slip or chipped one by setting it on the counter too quickly. As the kitchen men cheered them on, Pete's mounting stack of dried plates unnerved Elwood. The Texan had an edge on him, displaying new reserves. The onlookers made astonished noises. Elwood hurried, chasing after the image of the encyclopedias in their front room.

Len said, "Stop!"

Elwood won by one plate. The men hollered and laughed and traded glances whose meaning Elwood would interpret later.

Harold, one of the busboys, slapped Elwood on the back. "You were made to wash dishes, slick." The kitchen laughed.

Elwood returned volume *Aa–Be* to its box. It was a fancy reward.

"You earned it," Pete said. "I hope you get a lot of use out of them."

Elwood asked the housekeeping manager to tell his grandmother he was going home. He couldn't wait to see the look on her face when she saw the encyclopedias on their bookshelves, elegant and distinguished. Hunched, he dragged the boxes to the bus stop on Tennessee. To see him from across the street—the serious young lad heaving his freight of the world's knowledge—was to witness a scene that might have been illustrated by Norman Rockwell, if Elwood had had white skin.

At home, he cleared Hardy Boys and Tom Swifts from the

green bookcase in the front room and unpacked the boxes. He paused with *Ga*, curious to see how the smart men at the Fisher company handled *galaxy*. The pages were blank—all of them. Every volume in the first box was blank except for the one he'd seen in the kitchen. He opened the other two boxes, his face getting hot. All the books were empty.

When his grandmother came home, she shook her head and told him maybe they were defective, or dummy copies the salesman showed to customers as samples, so they could see how a full set would look in their homes. That night in bed his thoughts ticked and hummed like a contraption. It occurred to him that the busboy, that all the men in the kitchen had known the books were empty. That they had put on a show.

He kept the encyclopedias in the bookcase anyway. They looked impressive, even when the humidity peeled back the covers. The leather was fake, too.

The next afternoon in the kitchen was his last. Everyone paid too much attention to his face. Cory tested him with "How'd you like those books?" and waited for a reaction. Over by the sink Pete had a smile that looked as if it had been hacked into his jaw with a knife. They knew. His grandmother agreed that he was old enough to stay in the house by himself. Through high school, he went back and forth over the matter of whether the dishwashers had let him win all along. He'd been so proud of his ability, dumb and simple as it was. He never settled on one conclusion until he got to Nickel, which made the truth of the contests unavoidable.

CHAPTER TWO

Saying goodbye to the kitchen meant saying goodbye to his separate game, the one he kept private: Whenever the dining-room door swung open, he bet on whether there were Negro patrons out there. According to *Brown v. Board of Education*, schools had to desegregate—it was only a matter of time before all the invisible walls came down. The night the radio announced the Supreme Court's ruling, his grandmother shrieked as if someone had tossed hot soup in her lap. She caught herself and straightened her dress. "Jim Crow ain't going to just slink off," she said. "His wicked self."

The morning after the decision, the sun rose and everything looked the same. Elwood asked his grandmother when Negroes were going to start staying at the Richmond, and she said it's one thing to tell someone to do what's right and another thing for them to do it. She listed some of his behavior as proof and Elwood nodded: Maybe so. Sooner or later, though, the door would swing wide to reveal a brown face—a dapper businessman in Tallahassee for business or a fancy lady in town to see the sights—enjoying the fine-smelling fare the cooks put out. He was sure of it. The game began when he was nine, and three years later the only colored people he saw in the dining room carried plates or drinks or a mop. He never stopped playing, up until his afternoons at the Richmond ended. Whether his opponent in this game was his own foolishness or the mulish constancy of the world was unclear.

Mr. Parker was not the only one who saw a worthy employee in Elwood. White men were always extending offers of work to Elwood, recognizing his industrious nature and steady character, or at least recognizing that he carried himself differently than other colored boys his age and taking this for industry. Mr. Marconi, the proprietor of the tobacco shop on Macomb Street, had watched Elwood since he was a baby, squealing in a noisy carriage that was half rust. Elwood's mother was a slim woman with dark, tired eyes who never moved to quiet her child. She'd buy armfuls of movie magazines and vanish into the street, Elwood howling all the way.

Mr. Marconi left his perch by the register as seldom as possible. Squat and perspiring, with a low pompadour and a thin black mustache, he was inevitably disheveled by evening. The atmosphere at the front of the store was stringent with his hair tonic and he left an aromatic trail on hot afternoons. From his chair, Mr. Marconi observed Elwood grow older and lean toward his own sun, veering away from the neighborhood boys, who carried on and roughhoused in the aisles and slipped Red Hots into their dungarees when they thought Mr. Marconi wasn't looking. He saw everything, said nothing.

Elwood belonged to the second generation of his Frenchtown customers. Mr. Marconi hung out his shingle a few months after the army base opened in '42. Negro soldiers took the bus up from Camp Gordon Johnston or from Dale Mabry Army Air Field, raised hell in Frenchtown all weekend, then slumped back to train for war. He had relatives who opened businesses downtown and thrived, but a white man savvy to the economics of segregation could turn a real buck. Marconi's was a few doors down from the Bluebell Hotel. The Tip Top Bar and Marybelle's Pool Hall were around the corner. He did a reliable trade in various tobaccos and tins of Romeos prophylactics.

Once the war ended, he moved the cigars to the back of the store, repainted the walls white, and added magazine racks, penny candy, and a soda cooler, which did much to improve the place's reputation. He hired help. He didn't need an employee, but his wife liked telling people that he had an employee, and he imagined it made the store more approachable to a genteel segment of black Frenchtown.

Elwood was thirteen when Vincent, the tobacco shop's longtime stock boy, signed up for the army. Vincent hadn't been the most attentive employee, but he was prompt and well-groomed, two qualities that Mr. Marconi valued in others if not in himself. On Vincent's last day, Elwood dawdled at the comics rack, as he did most afternoons. He had a curious habit where he read every comic front to back before he bought it, and he bought every one he touched. Mr. Marconi asked why go through all that if he was going to buy them whether they were good or not, and Elwood said, "Just making sure." The shopkeeper asked him if he needed a job. Elwood closed the copy of *Journey into Mystery* and said he'd have to ask his grandmother.

Harriet had a long list of rules for what was acceptable and what was not, and sometimes the only way for Elwood to know how it all worked was to make a mistake. He waited until after dinner, once they'd finished the fried catfish and the sour greens and his grandmother rose to clear. In this case, she held no hidden reservations, despite the fact that her uncle Abe had smoked cigars and look what happened to him, despite Macomb Street's history as a laboratory of vice, and despite the fact she'd turned her mistreatment by an Italian salesclerk decades ago into a cherished grudge. "They're probably not related," she said, wiping her hands. "Or if they are, distant cousins."

She let Elwood work at the store after school and on weekends, taking half his paycheck at the end of the week for the household and half for college. He'd mentioned going to college the summer prior, casually, with no inkling of the momentousness of his words. *Brown v. Board of Education* was an unlikely turn, but one of Harriet's family aspiring to higher education was an actual miracle. Any misgivings over the tobacco shop collapsed before such a notion.

Elwood tidied the newspapers and comic books in the wire racks, wiped dust off the less popular sweets, and made sure that the cigar boxes were arranged according to Marconi's theories about packaging and how it excited "the happy part of the human brain." He still hung around the comics, reading them gingerly as if handling dynamite, but the news magazines exerted a gravity. He fell under the luxurious sway of *Life* magazine. A big white truck dropped off a stack of *Life* every Thursday—Elwood came to learn the sound of its brakes. Once he sorted the returns and displayed the new arrivals, he hunkered on the stepladder to follow the magazine's latest excursions into unreckoned corners of America.

He knew Frenchtown's piece of the Negro's struggle, where his neighborhood ended and white law took over. *Life*'s photo essays conveyed him to the front lines, to bus boycotts in Baton Rouge, to counter sit-ins in Greensboro, where young people not much older than him took up the movement. They were beaten with metal bars, blasted by fire hoses, spat on by white housewives with angry faces, and frozen by the camera in tableaus of noble resistance. The tiny details were a wonder: how the young men's ties remained straight black arrows in the whirl of violence, how the curves of the young women's perfect hairdos floated against the squares of their protest signs. Glamorous somehow, even when the blood flowed down their faces. Young knights taking the fight to dragons. Elwood was slight-shouldered, skinny as a pigeon, and he worried about the safety of his glasses, which were expensive and in his dreams broken in two by nightsticks, tire irons, or baseball bats, but he wanted to enlist. He had no choice.

Flipping pages during lulls. Elwood's shifts at Marconi's provided models for the man he wished to become and separated him from the type of Frenchtown boy he was not. His grandmother had long steered him from hanging out with the local kids, whom she regarded as shiftless, clambering into rambunction. The tobacco shop, like the hotel kitchen, was a safe preserve. Harriet raised him strict, everyone knew, and the other parents on their stretch of Brevard Street helped keep Elwood apart by holding him up as an example. When the boys he used to play cowboys and Indians with chased him down the street every once in a while or threw rocks at him, it was less out of mischief than resentment.

People from his block stopped in Marconi's all the time,

and his worlds overlapped. One afternoon, the bell above the door jangled and Mrs. Thomas walked in.

"Hello, Mrs. Thomas," Elwood said. "There's some cold orange in there."

"I think I just might, El," she said. A connoisseur of the latest styles, Mrs. Thomas was dressed this afternoon in a homemade yellow polka-dot dress she'd copied from a magazine profile of Audrey Hepburn. She was quite aware that few women in the neighborhood could have worn it with such confidence, and when she stood still it was hard to escape the suspicion that she was posing, waiting for the pop of flashbulbs.

Mrs. Thomas had been Evelyn Curtis's best friend growing up. One of Elwood's earliest memories was of sitting on his mother's lap on a hot day while they played gin. He squirmed to see his mother's cards and she told him not to fuss, it was too hot out. When she got up to visit the outhouse, Mrs. Thomas snuck him sips of her orange soda. His orange tongue gave them away and Evelyn half-heartedly scolded them while they giggled. Elwood kept that day close.

Mrs. Thomas opened her purse to pay for her two sodas and this week's *Jet*. "You keeping up with that schoolwork?"

"Yes, ma'am."

"I don't work the boy too hard," Mr. Marconi said.

"Mmm," Mrs. Thomas said. Her tone was suspect. Frenchtown ladies remembered the tobacco store from its disreputable days and considered the Italian an accomplice to domestic miseries. "You keep doing what you're supposed to, El." She took her change and Elwood watched her leave. His mother had left both of them; it was possible she sent her friend postcards from this or that place, even if she forgot to write him. One day Mrs. Thomas might share some news.

Mr. Marconi carried *Jet*, of course, and *Ebony*. Elwood got him to pick up *The Crisis* and *The Chicago Defender*, and other black newspapers. His grandmother and her friends subscribed, and he thought it strange that the store didn't sell them.

"You're right," Mr. Marconi said. He pinched his lip. "I think we used to carry it. I don't know what happened."

"Great," Elwood said.

Long after Mr. Marconi had stopped minding his regulars' buying habits, Elwood remembered what brought each person into the store. His predecessor, Vincent, had occasionally livened up the place with a dirty joke, but it couldn't be said that he had initiative. Elwood possessed it in spades, reminding Mr. Marconi which tobacco vendor had shorted them on the last delivery and which candy to quit restocking. Mr. Marconi struggled to tell the colored ladies of Frenchtown apart—all of them wore a scowl when they saw him—and Elwood made a competent ambassador. He'd stare at the boy when he was lost in his magazines and try to figure what made him tick. His grandmother was firm, that was clear. The boy was intelligent and hardworking and a credit to his race. But Elwood could be thick-witted when it came to the simplest things. He didn't know when to stand back and let things be. Like the business with the black eye.

Kids swiped candy, it didn't matter what color their skin was. Mr. Marconi himself, in his untethered youth, had engineered all sorts of foolishness. You lose a percentage here and there, but that was in the overhead—kids steal a candy bar today but they and their friends spend their money in the store for years. Them and their parents. Chase them out into the street over some little thing, word gets around, especially in a neighborhood like this where everybody's in everybody's business, and then the parents stop coming in because they're embarrassed. Letting the kids steal was almost an investment, the way he looked at it.

Elwood drifted to a different perspective during his time in the store. Before he worked at Marconi's, his friends gloated over their candy heists, cackling and blowing insolent pink bubbles of Bazooka once they got a good distance from the store. Elwood didn't join in but he'd never had feelings on it. When Mr. Marconi hired him, his boss explained his attitude toward sticky fingers, along with where they kept the mop and what days to expect the big deliveries. Over the months, Elwood saw sweets disappear into boys' pockets. Boys he knew. Maybe with a wink to Elwood if they caught his eye. For a year, Elwood said nothing. But the day Larry and Willie grabbed the lemon candies when Mr. Marconi bent behind the counter, he couldn't restrain himself.

"Put it back."

The boys stiffened. Larry and Willie had known Elwood their whole lives. Played marbles and tag with him when they were small, although that ended when Larry started a fire in the vacant lot on Dade Street and Willie got left back twice. Harriet struck them from the list of allowable companions. Their three families went back in Frenchtown for generations. Larry's grandmother was in a church group with Harriet, and Willie's father had been a childhood buddy of Elwood's father, Percy. They shipped off to the army together. Willie's father spent every day on his porch in his wheelchair, smoking a pipe, and he waved whenever Elwood passed.

"Put it back," Elwood said.

Mr. Marconi tilted his head: That's enough. The boys returned the candy and left the store, smoldering.

They knew Elwood's route. Sometimes jeered at him for being a goody-two-shoes when he biked past Larry's window on his way home. That night they jumped him. It was just getting dark and the smell of magnolias mingled with the tang of fried pork. They slammed him and his bike into the new asphalt the county had laid down that winter. The boys tore his sweater, threw his glasses into the street. As they beat him, Larry asked Elwood if he had any damned sense; Willie declared that he needed to be taught a lesson, and proceeded to do so. Elwood got a few licks in here and there, not much to talk about. He didn't cry. When he came upon two little kids fighting on his block, Elwood was the kind to intervene and cool things down. Now he was getting his. An old man from across the street broke it up and asked Elwood if he wanted to clean himself or have a glass of water. Elwood declined.

The chain on his bike was popped and he walked it home. Harriet didn't press him when she asked about his eye. He shook his head. By morning the livid bump underneath was a bubble of blood.

Larry had a point, Elwood had to admit: From time to time it appeared that he had no goddamned sense. He couldn't explain it, even to himself, until *At Zion Hill* gave him a language. *We must believe in our souls that we are somebody, that we are significant, that we are worthful, and we must walk the streets of life every day with this sense of dignity and this sense of somebody-ness.* The record went around and around, like an argument that always returned to its unassailable premise, and Dr. King's words filled the front room of the shotgun house. Elwood bent to a code—Dr. King gave that code shape, articulation, and meaning. There are big forces that want to keep the Negro down, like Jim Crow, and there are small forces that want to keep you down, like other people, and in the face of all those things, the big ones and the smaller ones, you have to stand up straight and maintain your sense of who you are. The encyclopedias are empty. There are people who trick you and deliver emptiness with a smile, while others rob you of your self-respect. You need to remember who you are.

This sense of dignity. The way the man said it, crackle and all: an inalienable strength. Even when consequences lay in wait on dark street corners on your way home. They beat him up and tore his clothes and didn't understand why he wanted to protect a white man. How to tell them that their transgressions against Mr. Marconi were insults to Elwood himself, whether it was a sucker candy or a comic book? Not because any attack on his brother was an attack on himself, like they said in church, but because for him to do nothing was to undermine his own dignity. No matter that Mr. Marconi had told him he didn't care, no matter that Elwood had never said a word to his friends when they stole in his presence. It didn't make no sense until it made the only sense.

That was Elwood—as good as anyone. On the day he was arrested, just before the deputy appeared, an advertisement for Fun Town came on the radio. He hummed along. He remembered that Yolanda King was six years old when her father told her the truth about the amusement park and the white order that kept her outside the fence looking in. Always looking into that other world. Elwood was six when his parents took off and he thought, that's another thing tying him to her, because that's when he woke to the world.

CHAPTER THREE

On the first day of the school year, the students of Lincoln High School received their new secondhand textbooks from the white high school across the way. Knowing where the textbooks were headed, the white students left inscriptions for the next owners: *Choke, Nigger! You Smell. Eat Shit.* September was a tutorial in the latest epithets of Tallahassee's white youth, which, like hemlines and haircuts, varied year to year. It was humiliating to open a biology book, turn to the page on the digestive system, and be confronted with *Drop dead NIGGER*, but as the school year went on, the students of Lincoln High School stopped noticing the curses and impolite suggestions. How to get through the day if every indignity capsized you in a ditch? One learned to focus one's attention.

Mr. Hill started working at the high school when Elwood entered his junior year. He greeted Elwood and the rest of the history class and wrote his name on the blackboard. Then Mr. Hill handed out black markers and told his students that the first order of business was to strike out all the bad words in the textbooks. "That always burned me up," he said, "seeing that stuff. You all are trying to get an education—no need to get caught up with what those fools say." Like the rest of the class, Elwood went slow at first. They looked at the textbooks and then at the teacher. Then they dug in with their markers. Elwood got giddy. His heart sped: this escapade. Why hadn't anyone told them to do this before?

"Make sure you don't miss anything," Mr. Hill said. "You know those white kids are wily." While the students struck out the curses and cusses, he told them about himself. He was new to Tallahassee, having just finished his studies at a teaching college in Montgomery. He'd first visited Florida the previous summer, when he stepped off a bus from Washington, DC, in Tallahassee as a freedom rider. He had marched. Installed himself at forbidden lunch counters and waited for service. "I got a lot of course work done," he said, "sitting there waiting for my cup of coffee." Sheriffs threw him in jail for breach of peace. He was almost bored as he shared these stories, as if what he had done was the most natural thing in the world. Elwood wondered if he'd seen him in the pages of *Life* or the *Defender*, arm in arm with the great movement leaders, or in the background with the anonymous ones, standing tall and proud.

Mr. Hill maintained a broad collection of bow ties: polka dot, bright red, banana yellow. His wide, kind face was somehow made kinder by the crescent scar over his right eye where a white man had slugged him with a tire iron. "Nashville," he said when someone asked one afternoon, and he bit into his pear. The class focused on US history since the Civil War, but at every opportunity Mr. Hill guided them to the present, linking what had happened a hundred years ago to their current lives. They'd set off down one road at the beginning of class and it always led back to their doorsteps.

Mr. Hill caught on that Elwood had a fascination with the rights struggle and gave the boy a wry smile when he chimed in. The rest of the faculty of Lincoln High School had long held the boy in high esteem, grateful for his cool temperament. Those who'd taught his parents years ago had a hard time squaring him—he may have carried his father's name but there was nothing in the boy of Percy's feral charm, or of Evelyn's unnerving gloom. Grateful was the teacher rescued by Elwood's contributions when the classroom fell drowsy with the afternoon heat and he offered up *Archimedes* or *Amsterdam* at the key moment. The boy had one usable volume of *Fisher's Universal Encyclopedia*, so he used it, what else could he do? Better than nothing. Skipping around, wearing it down, revisiting his favorite parts as if it were one of his adventure tales. As a story, the encyclopedia was disjointed and incomplete, but still exciting in its own right. Elwood filled his notebook with the good parts, definitions and etymology. Later he'd find this scrap-rummaging pathetic.

He had been the natural choice at the end of his freshman year when they needed a new lead for the annual Emancipation Day play. Playing Thomas Jackson, the man who informs the Tallahassee slaves that they are free, was training for the version of himself who lived up the road. Elwood invested the character with the same earnestness he brought to all his responsibilities. In the play, Thomas Jackson was a cutter on a sugar plantation who ran away to join the Union Army at the start of the war, returning home a statesman. Every year Elwood concocted new inflections and gestures, the speeches losing their stiffness as his own convictions enlivened the portrait. "It is my pleasure to inform you fine gentlemen and ladies that the time has come to throw off the yoke of slavery and take our places as true Americans—at long last!" The play's author, a teacher of biology, had attempted to summon the magic of her one trip to Broadway years before.

In the three years Elwood played the role, the one constant was his nervousness at the climax, when Jackson had to kiss his best girl on the cheek. They were to be married and, it was implied, live a happy and fertile life in the new Tallahassee. Whether Marie-Jean was played by Anne, with her freckles and sweet moon face, or by Beatrice, whose buck teeth hooked into her lower lip, or in his final performance by Gloria Taylor, a foot taller and sending him to the tips of his toes, a knot of anxiety tautened in his chest and he got dizzy. All the hours in Marconi's library had rehearsed him for heavy speeches but left him ill-prepared for performances with the brown beauties of Lincoln High, on the stage and off.

The movement he read and fantasized about was far off—then it crept closer. Frenchtown had its protests, but Elwood was too young to join in. He was ten years old when the two girls from Florida A&M University proposed the bus boycott. His grandmother initially didn't understand why they wanted to bring all that fuss to their city, but after a few days she was carpooling to the hotel like everyone else. "Everybody in Leon County has gone crazy," she said, "including me!" That winter the city finally integrated the buses and she got on and saw a colored driver behind the wheel. Sat where she wanted.

Four years later, when the students got it in their mind to sit down at the lunch counter at Woolworths, Elwood remembered his grandmother cackling with approval. She even gave fifty cents to support their legal defense after the sheriff jailed them. When the demonstrations trailed off, she continued to boycott downtown stores, although it was not clear how much of that was solidarity or her own protest against high prices. In the spring of '63, word spread that the college kids were going to picket the Florida Theatre to open its seats to Negroes. Elwood had good reason to think that Harriet would be proud of him for stepping up.

He was incorrect. Harriet Johnson was a slight hummingbird of a woman who conducted herself in everything with furious purpose. If something was worth doing—working, eating, talking to another person—it was worth doing seriously or not at all. She kept a sugarcane machete under her pillow for intruders, and it was difficult for Elwood to think that the old woman was afraid of anything. But fear was her fuel.

Yes, Harriet had joined the bus boycott. She had to—she couldn't be the only woman in Frenchtown to take public transportation. But she trembled each time Slim Harrison pulled up in his '57 Cadillac and she squeezed into the back with the other downtown-bound ladies. When the sit-ins started, she was grateful that no one expected a public gesture on her part. Sit-ins were a young person's game and she didn't have the heart. Act above your station, and you will pay. Whether it was God angry at her for taking more than her portion or the white man teaching her not to ask for more crumbs than he wanted to give, Harriet would pay. Her father had paid for not stepping out of the way of a white lady on Tennessee Avenue. Her husband, Monty, paid when he stepped up. Elwood's father, Percy, got too many ideas when he joined the army so that when he came back there was no room in Tallahassee for everything in his head. Now, Elwood. She'd bought that Martin Luther King record from a salesman outside the Richmond for a dime and it was the damnedest ten cents she'd ever handed over. That record was nothing but ideas.

Hard work was a fundamental virtue, for hard work didn't allow time for marches or sit-ins. Elwood would not make a commotion of himself by messing with that movie-theater nonsense, she said. "You have made an agreement with Mr. Marconi to work in his store after school. If your boss can't depend on you, you won't be able to keep a job." Duty might protect him, as it had protected her.

A cricket under the house made a racket. Should've been paying rent, it had been flopping with them for so long. Elwood looked up from his science book and said, "Okay." The next afternoon he asked Mr. Marconi for a day off. Elwood had been out sick two days, but apart from that and some visits to see family, he hadn't missed work in those three years at the store.

Mr. Marconi said sure. Didn't even look up from his racing form.

Elwood dressed in the dark slacks from last year's Emancipation Day play. He'd grown a few inches, so he let them out and they showed the barest sliver of his white socks. A new emerald tie clip held his black tie in place and the knot only took six attempts. His shoes glinted with polish. He looked the part, even if he still worried for his glasses if the police brought out nightsticks. If the whites carried iron pipes and baseball bats. He waved off the bloody images from newspapers and magazines and tucked in his shirt.

Elwood heard the chants when he reached the Esso station on Monroe. "What do we want? Freedom! When do we want it? Now!" The A&M students marched in snaky loops in front of the Florida, hoisting signs and rotating slogans under the marquee. The theater was showing *The Ugly American*—if you had seventy-five cents and the right skin color, you could see Marlon Brando. The sheriff and his deputies had installed themselves on the sidewalk in dark sunglasses, arms crossed. A group of whites jeered and taunted behind the policemen, and more white men trotted down the street to join them. Elwood kept his eyes down as he walked around the mob and slipped into the protest line behind an older girl in a striped sweater. She grinned at him and nodded as if she had been waiting for him.

He calmed once he joined the human chain and mouthed the words with the others. EQUAL TREATMENT UNDER THE LAW. Where was his sign? In his concentration on looking the part, he'd forgotten his props. He couldn't have matched the older kids' perfect stencil work. They'd had practice. NONVIOLENCE IS OUR WATCHWORD. WE SHALL WIN BY LOVE. A short boy with a shaved head waved one that said, ARE YOU THE UGLY AMERICAN in a sea of cartoony question marks. Someone grabbed Elwood's shoulder. He thought he'd see a monkey wrench bearing down, but it was Mr. Hill. His history teacher invited him into a group of Lincoln seniors. Bill Tuddy and Alvin Tate, two guys from varsity basketball, shook his hand. They'd never acknowledged him before. He'd kept his movement dreams so close that it never occurred to him that others in his school shared his need to stand up.

The next month the sheriff arrested more than two hundred protestors and charged them with contempt, snatching collars in a roil of tear gas, but this first march went off without incident. By then the FAMU students would be joined by those from Melvin Griggs Technical. White kids from the University of Florida and Florida State. Skilled hands from the Congress of Racial Equality. This day, old and young white men shouted at them, but it was nothing Elwood hadn't heard shouted from cars when biking down the street. One of the red-faced white boys looked like Cameron Parker, the son of the Richmond's manager, and the next circuit confirmed it. They'd traded comic books a few years ago in the alley behind the hotel. Cameron didn't recognize him. A flashbulb exploded in his face and Elwood started, but the photographer was from the *Register*, which his grandmother refused to read because their race coverage was so slanted. A college girl in a tight blue sweater handed him a sign that said I AM A MAN and when the protest moved to the State Theatre, he held it over his head and lent his voice to the proud chorus. The State was playing *The Day Mars Invaded Earth* and that night he thought he'd traveled a hundred thousand miles in one day.

Three days later Harriet confronted him—one of her circle had seen him and that's how long it took for the news to get back to her. It had been years since she spanked him with a belt and now he was much too big, so she resorted to an old Johnson family recipe for the silent treatment, one that dated back to Reconstruction and achieved a complete sense of erasure in its target. She instituted a ban on the record player and, recognizing the resiliency of this younger generation of colored youth, moved it into her bedroom and weighed it down with bricks. They both suffered in the quiet.

After a week, things in the house were back to their routine, but Elwood was changed. *Closer.* At the demonstration, he had felt somehow *closer* to himself. For a moment. Out there in the sun. It was enough to feed his dreams. Once he got to college and out of their little shotgun house on Brevard, he'd start his life. Take girls to the movies—he was done stymieing himself on that front—and figure out a course of study. Find his place in the busy line of young dreamers who dedicated themselves to Negro uplift.

That last summer in Tallahassee passed quickly. Mr. Hill gave him a copy of James Baldwin's *Notes of a Native Son* on the last day of school, and his mind churned. *Negroes are Americans and their destiny is the country's destiny.* He hadn't marched on the Florida Theatre in defense of his rights or those of the black race of which he was a part; he had marched for everyone's rights, even those who shouted him down. My struggle is your struggle, your burden is my burden. But how to tell people? He stayed up late writing letters on the racial question to the *Tallahassee Register,* which did not run them, and *The Chicago Defender,* which printed one. "We ask of the older generation, Will you pick up our challenge?" Bashful, he didn't tell anyone and wrote under a pseudonym: Archer Montgomery. It sounded stuffy and smart, and he didn't realize he'd used his grandfather's name until he saw it in black-and-white newsprint.

In June Mr. Marconi became a grandfather, a milestone that exposed new facets in the Italian. He turned the shop into a showcase for avuncular enthusiasm. The long silences gave way to lessons from his immigrant struggles and eccentric business advice. He took to closing the shop an hour early to visit his granddaughter and paid Elwood for a full shift. When this happened, Elwood strolled over to the basketball courts to see if anyone was playing. He only ever watched, but his excursion to the protests had made him less shy and he made a few friends on the sidelines, dudes from two streets over whom he'd seen for years but never talked to. Other times he might go downtown with Peter Coombs, a neighborhood boy Harriet approved of on account that he played violin and shared a bookish bent with her grandson. If Peter didn't have practice, they wandered the record stores and furtively checked out the covers of LPs they were forbidden to buy.

"What's 'Dynasound'?" Peter asked.

A new style of music? A different way of hearing? They were confounded.

Once in a while on hot afternoons girls from FAMU stopped in the store for a soda, someone from the Florida demonstration. Elwood asked for news on the protests, and they'd brighten at the connection and pretend to recognize him. More than one told him that they assumed he was in college. He took their observations as compliments, ornaments on his daydreams about leaving home. Optimism made Elwood as malleable as the cheap taffy below the register. He was primed when Mr. Hill appeared in the store that July and made his suggestion.

Elwood didn't recognize him at first. No colorful bow tie, an orange plaid shirt open to show his undershirt, hip sunglasses—Mr. Hill looked like someone who hadn't thought about work for months, not weeks. He greeted his former student with the lazy ease of someone who had the whole summer off. For the first summer in a while he wasn't traveling, he told Elwood. "There's plenty here to keep me occupied," he said, nodding toward the sidewalk. A young woman in a floppy straw hat waited for him, her thin hand shading her eyes from the sunlight.

Elwood asked Mr. Hill if he needed anything.

"I came here to see you, Elwood," he said. "A friend of mine told me about an opportunity and I thought of you right off the bat."

Mr. Hill had a comrade from the freedom riders, a college professor who'd landed a job at Melvin Griggs Technical, the colored college just south of Tallahassee. Teaching English and American literature, just finished his third year. The school had been poorly managed for some time; the new president of the college was turning things around. The courses at Melvin Griggs had been open to high-achieving high-school students for some time, but none of the local families knew about it. The president put Mr. Hill's friend on it, and he reached out: Perhaps there were a few exceptional kids at Lincoln who might be interested?

Elwood tightened his hands on the broom. "That sounds great, but I don't know if we have the money for classes like that." Later, he'd shake his head: College classes were exactly what he'd been saving up for, what did it matter if he took them while still at Lincoln?

"That's the thing, Elwood—they're free. This fall at least, so they can get the word out in the community."

"I'll have to ask my grandmother."

"You do that, Elwood," Mr. Hill said. "And I can talk to her, too." He put his hand on Elwood's shoulder. "The main thing is, it'd be perfect for a young man like you. You're the type of student they came up with this for."

Later that afternoon as he chased a fat, buzzing fly around the store, Elwood thought there probably weren't a lot of white kids in Tallahassee who studied at the college level.

He who gets behind in a race must forever remain behind or run faster than the man in front.

Harriet expressed no misgivings over Mr. Hill's offer—the word *free* was a master switch. After that, Elwood's summer moved as slow as a mud turtle. Because Mr. Hill's friend taught English, he thought he had to sign up for a literature course, but even when he found out he could take anything he wanted, he stuck with it. The survey course on British writers wasn't practical, as his grandmother pointed out, but that was its charm, the more he thought about it. He had been exceedingly practical for a long time.

Perhaps the textbooks at the college might be new. Unscarred. Nothing to cross out. It was possible.

The day before Elwood's first college class, Mr. Marconi summoned him to the cash register. Elwood had to miss his Thursday shifts in order to attend; he assumed his boss wanted to make sure things were in order for his absence. The Italian cleared his throat and pushed a velvet case to him. "For your education," he said.

It was a midnight-blue fountain pen with brass trim. A nice gift, even if Mr. Marconi got a discount because the stationers were a steady client. They shook hands in a manly fashion.

Harriet wished him good luck. She checked his school outfit every morning to make sure he was presentable, but apart from plucking the occasional piece of lint never made any corrections. This day was no different. "You look smart, El," she said. She kissed him on the cheek before heading to the bus stop, hunching her shoulders in the way she did when she was trying not to cry in front of him.

Elwood had plenty of time after school to get to the college, but he was so eager to see Melvin Griggs for the first time that he set out early. Two rivets in his bike chain broke the night he got that black eye, and ever since it tended to snap when he took it out for long rides. He'd stick out his thumb or walk the seven miles. Step through the gates and explore the campus, get lost in all those buildings, or just sit on a bench off the quadrangle and breathe it in.

He waited at the corner of Old Bainbridge for a colored driver who headed for the state road. Two pickups passed him by and then a brilliant-green '61 Plymouth Fury slowed, low and finned like a giant catfish. The driver leaned over and opened the passenger door. "Going south," he said. The green-and-white vinyl seats squeaked when Elwood slid inside.

"Rodney," the man said. Rodney had a sprawling but solid physique, like a Negro version of Edward G. Robinson. His gray-and-purple pinstripe suit completed the costume. When Rodney shook his hand, the rings on his fingers bit and made Elwood wince.

"Elwood." He put his satchel between his legs and looked over the space-age dashboard of the Plymouth, all the push buttons sticking out of the silver detailing.

They headed south toward County Road 636. Rodney tapped vainly at the radio. "This always gives me trouble. You try it." Elwood stabbed the buttons and found an R&B station. He almost turned the channel, but Harriet wasn't here to cluck over the double meanings in the lyrics, her explanations of which always left him mystified and dubious. He let the station sit, it was a doo-wop group. Rodney wore the same hair tonic as Mr. Marconi. The air in the car was acrid and heavy with the stuff. Even on his day off, he couldn't rid himself of it.

Rodney was on his way back from seeing his mother, who

lived in Valdosta. He said he hadn't heard of Melvin Griggs before, putting a dent in Elwood's pride over his big day. "College," Rodney said. He whistled through his teeth. "I started working in a chair factory when I was fourteen," he added.

"I have a job in a tobacco store," Elwood said.

"I'm sure you do," Rodney said.

The disc jockey rattled off the information for the Sunday swap meet. A commercial for Fun Town came on and Elwood hummed along.

"What's this?" Rodney said. He exhaled loudly and cursed. Ran his hand over his conk.

The red light of the prowl car spun in the rearview mirror.

They were in the country and there were no other cars. Rodney muttered and pulled over. Elwood put his satchel in his lap and Rodney told him to keep cool.

The white deputy parked a few yards behind them. He put his left hand on his holster and walked up. He took off his sunglasses and put them in his chest pocket.

Rodney said, "You don't know me, do you?"

"No," Elwood said.

"I'll tell him that."

The deputy had his gun out now. "First thing I thought when they said to keep an eye out for a Plymouth," he said. "Only a nigger'd steal that."

PART Two

CHAPTER FOUR

After the judge ordered him to Nickel, Elwood had three last nights at home. The state car arrived at seven o'clock Tuesday morning. The officer of the court was a good old boy with a meaty backwoods beard and a hungover wobble to his step. He'd outgrown his shirt and the pressure against the buttons made him look upholstered. But he was a white man with a pistol so despite his dishevelment he sent a vibration. Along the street men watched from porches and smoked and gripped the railings as if afraid of falling overboard. The neighbors peeked through their windows for a view, connecting the scene to events from years before, when a boy or a man was taken away and he was not someone who lived across the street but kin. Brother, son.

The officer tossed a toothpick around in his mouth when he talked, which was not often. He handcuffed Elwood to a metal bar that ran behind the front seat and didn't speak for two hundred and seventy-five miles.

They got down to Tampa and five minutes later the officer was in a fight with the clerk at the jail. There had been a mistake: All three boys were headed for the Nickel Academy, and the colored boy was supposed to be picked up last, not first. Tallahassee was only an hour away from the school after all. Didn't he think it strange that he was driving the boy up and down the state like a yo-yo, the clerk asked? At this point his face was red.

"I just read what's on the paper," the officer said.

"It's alphabetical," the clerk said.

Elwood rubbed at the mark the cuffs cut into his wrists and could have sworn the bench in the waiting room was a church pew, it was the same shape.

Half an hour later they were on the road again. Franklin T. and Bill Y.: alphabetically distant and temperamentally even farther. Elwood took the two white boys next to him for rough characters from the first scowl. Franklin T. had the most freckled face he'd ever seen, with a deep suntan and crew-cut red hair. He had a downcast look, head sunk, staring at his toes, but when he lifted his eyes to other people they were invariably vesseled with fury. Bill Y.'s eyes, for their part, had been punched black, purple, and lurid. His lips were puffed and scabbed. The brown, pear-shaped birthmark on his right cheek added another hue to his mottled face. He snorted when he got a look at Elwood, and whenever their legs touched on the drive, Bill pulled back as if he'd leaned against a hot chimney stove.

Whatever their life stories, whatever they'd done to get sent to Nickel, the boys were chained together in the same fashion and headed to the same destination. Franklin and Bill exchanged notes after a while. This was Franklin's second visit to Nickel. The first time was for being recalcitrant; he was back for truancy. He got a licking for eyeballing the wife of one of the house fathers, but other than that the place was decent, he supposed. Away from his stepfather at least. Bill was being raised by his sister and fell in with a bunch of bad apples, as the judge put it. They broke the front window of a pharmacy, but Bill got off easy. He was going to Nickel because he was only fourteen, while the rest were heading up to Piedmont.

The officer told the white boys that they were sitting with a car thief and Bill laughed. "Oh, I used to go joyriding all the time," he said. "They should have pinched me for that, not some dumb window."

Outside of Gainesville they drifted off the interstate. The officer pulled over to let everyone piss and gave them mustard sandwiches. He didn't cuff them when they got back in the car. The officer said he knew they weren't going to run. He skirted Tallahassee, taking the back road around it like the place didn't exist anymore. I don't even recognize the trees, Elwood told himself when they got to Jackson County. Feeling low.

He got a look at the school and thought maybe Franklin was right—Nickel wasn't that bad. He expected tall stone walls and barbed wire, but there were no walls at all. The campus was kept up meticulously, a bounty of lush green dotted with two- and three-story buildings of red brick. The cedar trees and beeches cut out portions of shade, tall and ancient. It was the nicest-looking property Elwood had ever seen—a real school, a good one, not the forbidding reformatory he'd conjured the last few weeks. In a sad joke, it intersected with his visions of Melvin Griggs Technical, minus a few statues and columns.

They drove up the long road to the main administration building and Elwood caught sight of a football field where some boys scrimmaged and yelped. In his head he'd seen kids attached to balls and chains, something out of cartoons, but these fellows were having a swell time out there, thundering around the grass.

"All right," Bill said, pleased. Elwood was not the only one reassured.

The officer said, "Don't get smart. If the housemen don't run you down, and the swamp don't suck you up—"

"They call in those dogs from the state penitentiary, Apalachee," Franklin said.

"You get along and you'll get along," the officer said.

Inside the building the officer waved down a secretary who took them into a yellow room whose walls were lined with wooden filing cabinets. The chairs were in classroom rows and the boys picked spots far apart from one another. Elwood took a place in the front, per his custom. They all sat up when Superintendent Spencer knocked the door open.

Maynard Spencer was a white man in his late fifties, bits of silver in his cropped black hair. A real "crack of dawner," as Harriet used to say, who moved with a deliberate air, as if he rehearsed everything in front of a mirror. He had a narrow raccoon face that drew Elwood's attention to his tiny nose and dark circles under his eyes and thick bristly eyebrows. Spencer was fastidious with his dark blue Nickel uniform; every crease in his clothes looked sharp enough to cut, as if he were a living blade.

Spencer nodded at Franklin, who grabbed the corners of his desk. The supervisor suppressed a smile, as if he'd known the boy would be back. He leaned against the blackboard and crossed his arms. "You got here late in the day," he said, "so I won't go on too long. Everybody's here because they haven't figured out how to be around decent people. That's okay. This is a school, and we're teachers. We're going to teach you how to do things like everyone else.

"I know you heard all this before, Franklin, but it didn't take, obviously. Maybe this time it will. Right now, all of you are Grubs. We have four ranks of behavior here—start as a Grub, work your way up to Explorer, then Pioneer, and finally, Ace. Earn merits for acting right, and you move on up the ladder. You work on achieving the highest rank of Ace and then you graduate and go home to your families." He paused. "If they'll have you, but that's between y'all." An Ace, he said, listens to the housemen and his house father, does his work without shirking and malingering, and applies himself to his studies. An Ace does not rough-house, he does not cuss, he does not blaspheme or carry on. He works to reform himself, from sunrise to sunset. "It's up to you how much time you spend with us," Spencer said. "We don't mess around with idiots here. If you mess up, we have a place for you, and you will not like it. I'll see to it personally."

Spencer had a severe face, but when he touched the enormous key ring on his belt the corners of his mouth twitched in pleasure, it seemed, or to signal a murkier emotion. The supervisor turned to Franklin, the boy who'd come back for a second taste of Nickel. "Tell them, Franklin."

Franklin's voice cracked and he had to fix himself before he got out, "Yes, sir. You don't want to step over the line in here."

The supervisor looked at each boy in turn, took notes in his head, and stood. "Mr. Loomis will finish processing you," he said, and walked out. The ring of keys on his belt jangled like spurs on a sheriff in a Western.

A sullen young white man—Loomis—appeared minutes later and led them to the basement room where they kept the school uniforms. Denim pants, gray work shirts, and brown brogues in different sizes filled shelves on the walls. Loomis told the boys to find their sizes, directing Elwood to the colored section, which contained the more-threadbare items. They changed into their new clothes. Elwood folded his shirt and dungarees and put them in the canvas sack he'd brought from home. He had two sweaters in the bag, and his suit from the Emancipation Day play, for church. Franklin and Bill hadn't brought anything with them.

Elwood tried not to stare at the marks on the other boys' bodies as they dressed. Both of them had long lumpy lines of scars and what looked like burn marks. He never saw Franklin and Bill after that day. The school had more than six hundred students; the white boys went down the hill and the black boys went up the hill.

Back in the intake room, the boys waited for their house fathers to fetch them. Elwood's arrived first, a chubby, white-haired man with dark skin and gray, mirthful eyes. Where Spencer was severe and intimidating, Blakeley's personality was soft and pleasant. He gave Elwood a warm handshake and told him that he was in charge of his assigned dormitory, Cleveland.

They walked to the colored housing. Elwood's posture unscrewed. He was scared of a place that was run by men like Spencer and what that meant for his time there—to be under the eyes of men who liked to make threats and relished the effect of their threats on people—but perhaps the black staff looked after their own. And even if they were just as mean as the white men, Elwood had never permitted himself the kind of misbehavior that landed others in trouble. He consoled himself with the notion that he just had to keep doing what he'd always done: act right.

There weren't many students out and about. Figures moved in the windows of the residential buildings. Dinnertime, Elwood supposed. The few black boys who passed them on the concrete walkway greeted Blakeley with respect and didn't see Elwood at all.

Blakeley said he'd worked at the school for eleven years, from the "bad old days up to now." The school had a philosophy, he explained, in that they put the boys' fates in their own hands. "You boys are in charge of everything," Blakeley said. "Burn the bricks in all these buildings you see here, lay the concrete, take care of all this grass. Do a good job, too, as you can see." Work keeps the boys level, he continued, provides skills they can use when they graduate. Nickel's printing press did all the publishing for the government of Florida, from the tax regulations to the building codes to the parking tickets. "Learn how to execute those big orders and take your corner of responsibility, that's knowledge you can draw on for the rest of your life."

Every boy had to attend school, Blakeley said, that was a rule. Other reformatory schools might not strike that balance between reform and education, but Nickel made sure that their charges did not fall behind, with classroom instruction every other day, alternating with work details, Sundays off.

The house father noticed the change in Elwood's expression. "Not what you expected?"

"I was going to take college classes this year," Elwood said. It was October; he would have been deep into the semester.

"Speak to Mr. Goodall about it," Blakeley said. "He teaches the older students. I'm sure you can come to an arrangement." He smiled. "You ever worked a field?" he asked. They grew multiple crops on the 1,400 acres—limes, sweet potatoes, watermelon. "I came up on a farm," Blakeley said. "A lot of these kids, it's their first time taking care of anything."

"Yes, sir," Elwood said. There was a tag or something in his shirt; it kept sticking him in the neck.

Blakeley stopped. He said, "You know when to say, *Yes, sir*—which is always—you'll be okay, son." He was familiar with Elwood's "situation"—his intonation swaddled the word in euphemism. "A lot of the boys here, they got in over their heads. This is an opportunity to take stock and get your head right."

Cleveland was identical to the other dormitories on the campus: Nickel brick under a green copper roof, surrounded by box hedges that clawed out of the red soil. Blakeley took Elwood through the front door and it was swiftly clear that outside was one thing and inside another. The warped floors creaked incessantly and the yellow walls were scuffed and scratched. Stuffing dribbled from the couches and armchairs in the recreation room. Initials and epithets marked the tables, gouged by a hundred mischievous hands. Elwood fixated on the housekeeping chores Harriet would have ticked off for his attention: the fuzzy haloes of finger grime around every cabinet latch and doorknob, the balls of dirt and hair in the corners.

Blakeley explained the layout. The first floor of each dorm was taken up by a small kitchen, the administration offices, and two large assembly rooms. On the second were the dorm rooms, two of them for the high-school-age students and one reserved for the younger kids. "We call the younger students 'chucks,' but don't ask me why—nobody knows." On the top was where Blakeley lived and some utility rooms. The boys were heading to bed, Blakeley told him. The dining hall was a walk and they were wrapping up supper, but did he want something from the kitchen before they closed for the night? Elwood couldn't think of food, he was too knotted up.

There was an empty bed in room 2. Three rows of bunks stretched over the blue linoleum, each row with ten beds, each bed with a trunk at the foot for the boy's things. No one had paid Elwood any attention on the walk over, but in here each boy took his measure, some of them conferring quietly with their buddies as Blakeley took him down the rows and others filing away their appraisals for later. One boy looked like a thirty-year-old man, but Elwood knew that was impossible since they let you out when you turned eighteen. Some of the boys carried themselves rough, like the white boys in the car from Tampa, but he was relieved that a lot of them looked like regular guys from his neighborhood, just sadder. If they were regular, he'd make it through.

Despite what he'd heard, Nickel was indeed a school and not a grim jail for juveniles. Elwood had gotten off lucky, his lawyer said. Stealing a car was a big-ticket offense for Nickel. He'd learn that most of the kids had been sent here for much lesser—and nebulous and inexplicable—offenses. Some students were wards of the state, without family, and there was nowhere else to put them.

Blakeley opened the trunk to show Elwood his soap and towel, and introduced him to the boys who slept on either side of him, Desmond and Pat. The house father instructed them to show Elwood the ropes: "Don't think I won't be watching you." The two boys mumbled hello and returned to their baseball cards once Blakeley disappeared.

Elwood had never been much of a crier, but he'd taken it up since the arrest. The tears came at night, when he imagined what Nickel held in store for him. When he heard his grandmother sobbing in her room next door, fussing around, opening and closing things because she didn't know what to do with her hands. When he tried without success to figure out why his life had bent to this wretched avenue. He knew he couldn't let the boys see him weep, so he turned over in the bunk and put his pillow over his head and listened to the voices: the jokes and taunts, the stories of home and distant cronies, the juvenile conjectures about how the world worked and their naïve plans to outwit it.

He'd started the day in his old life and ended it here. The pillowcase smelled like vinegar, and in the night the katydids and crickets screeched in waves, soft then loud, back and forth.

Elwood was asleep when a different roar commenced. It came from outside, a rush and a whoosh without variation. Forbidding and mechanical and granting no clue to its origin. He didn't know which book he'd picked it up from, but the word came to him: *torrential.*

A voice across the room said, "Somebody's going out for ice cream," and a few boys snickered.

CHAPTER FIVE

Elwood met Turner his second day at Nickel, which was also the day he discovered the grim purpose of the noise. "Most niggers last whole weeks before they go down," the boy named Turner told him later. "You got to quit that eager-beaver shit, El."

A bugler and his brisk reveille woke them most mornings. Blakeley rapped on the door of room 2 and yelled, "Time to get up!" The students saluted another morning at Nickel with groans and cussing. They lined up two by two for attendance, and then came the two-minute shower where the boys furiously lathered with the chalky soap before their time ran out. Elwood put on a good show of acting unsurprised by the communal showers but had less success hiding his horror at the frigid water, which was searching and merciless. What came from the pipes smelled of rotten eggs, as did anyone who bathed in it until their skin dried.

"Now it's breakfast," Desmond said. His bunk was next to Elwood's and the boy made an effort to fulfill the house father's orders from the night before. Desmond had a round head, chubby baby cheeks, and a voice that startled everyone the first time they heard it, it was so gruff and full of bass. His voice made the chucks jump when he crept up on them, and he got a kick out of it, until one day a supervisor with an even deeper voice crept up on him and taught him a lesson.

Elwood told him his name again, to signal a new start to their acquaintance.

"You told me last night," Desmond said. He laced his brown shoes, which were impeccably polished. "If you've been here a while, you're supposed to help out the Grubs, so you can get points. I'm halfway to Pioneer."

He walked with Elwood the quarter mile to the dining hall, but they got separated in the chow line, and when Elwood looked for a place to sit he didn't see him. The mess hall was loud and rowdy, full of all the Cleveland boys serving up their morning round of nonsense. Elwood was invisible again. He found an empty seat at one of the long tables. When he neared, a boy slapped his hand on the bench and said it was saved. The next table over was filled with younger kids but when Elwood put his tray down they looked at him like he was crazy. "Big kids aren't allowed to sit at a little-kids table," one of them said.

Elwood sat down quickly at the next free spot he saw and to head off rebuke didn't make eye contact, just ate. The oatmeal had a bunch of cinnamon dumped into it to hide a lousy taste. Elwood gobbled it down. He finished peeling his orange before he finally looked up at the boy across the table who had been staring at him.

The first thing Elwood noticed was the notch in the boy's left ear, like on an alley cat that had been in scrapes. The boy said, "You eat that oatmeal like your mama made it."

Who was this, talking about his mother. "What?"

He said, "I didn't mean it like that, I meant I ain't never seen someone eat this food like that—like they liked it."

The second thing Elwood noticed was the boy's eerie sense of self. The mess hall was loud with the rumble and roil of juvenile activity, but this boy bobbed in his own pocket of calm. Over time, Elwood saw that he was always simultaneously at home in whatever scene he found himself and also seemed like he shouldn't have been there; inside and above at the same time; a part and apart. Like a tree trunk that falls across a creek—it doesn't belong and then it's never not been there, generating its own ripples in the larger current.

He said his name was Turner.

"I'm Elwood. From Tallahassee. Frenchtown."

"Frenchtown." A boy down the line mimicked Elwood's voice, giving it a sissy turn, and his buddies laughed.

There were three of them. The biggest one he'd seen last night, the boy who looked too old to attend Nickel. The giant was named Griff; in addition to his mature appearance, he was broad-chested and hunched like a big brown bear. Griff's daddy, it was said, was on a chain gang in Alabama for murdering his mother, making his meanness a handed-down thing. Griff's two pals were Elwood's size, lean on the bone but wild and cruel in the eyes. Lonnie's wide bulldog face tapered into a bullet at his shaved scalp. He'd scrounged up a patchy mustache and had a habit of smoothing it with his thumb and index finger when calculating brutality. The last member of the trio was called Black Mike. He was a wiry youth from Opelousas who was in constant battle with restless blood; this morning he wobbled in his seat and sat on his hands to keep them from flying off. The three of them owned the other end of the table—the seats between were empty because everyone else knew better.

"I don't know why you so loud, Griff," Turner said. "You knew they got their eye on you this week."

Elwood assumed he meant the housemen; there were eight of them spread out at different tables in the mess, eating with their charges. It was impossible he'd overheard, but the houseman closest to them looked up and sent everybody act-casual. Griff, the bruiser, made a barking noise at Turner and the other two boys laughed, the dog noises part of a running gag. The one with the shaved head, Lonnie, winked at Elwood and then they returned to their morning meeting.

"I'm from Houston myself," Turner said. He sounded bored. "That's a real city. None of this country shit y'all got up here."

"Thanks for that," Elwood said. He tipped his head toward the bullies.

The boy picked up his tray. "I didn't do shit."

Then everyone was on their feet: Time for class. Desmond tapped Elwood on the shoulder and escorted him. The colored schoolhouse was down the hill, next to the garage and the warehouse. "I used to hate school," Desmond said. "But here you can grab some shut-eye."

"I thought this place was strict," Elwood said.

"Back home, my daddy'd beat my ass if I missed a day of school. Nickel, though." Academic performance had no bearing on one's progress to graduation, Desmond explained. Teachers didn't take attendance or hand out grades. The clever kids worked on their merits. Enough merits and you could get an early release for good behavior. Work, comportment, demonstrations of compliance or docility, however—these things counted toward your ranking and were never far from Desmond's attention. He had to get home. He was from Gainesville, where his father had a shoeshine stand. Desmond took off so many times, raising hell, that his father begged Nickel to take him. "I was sleeping under the stars so much, he thought I'd learn to appreciate having a roof over my head."

Elwood asked him if it was working.

Desmond turned away and said, "Man, I got to make it to Pioneer." His grown-up man's voice, coming out of his scrawny body, made it a poignant wish.

The colored schoolhouse was older than the dormitories, one of the few structures that dated back to the opening of the school. There were two classrooms upstairs for the chucks and two on the main floor for the older kids. Desmond steered Elwood into their homeroom, which had fifty desks or so crammed inside. Elwood squeezed into the second row and was swiftly appalled. The posters on the walls featured bespectacled owls hooting out the alphabet next to bright drawings of elementary nouns: house, cat, barn. Little-kid stuff. Worse than the secondhand textbooks at Lincoln High, all the Nickel textbooks were from before he was born, earlier editions of textbooks Elwood remembered from first grade.

The teacher Mr. Goodall appeared, but no one paid him any mind. Goodall was a pink-skinned man in his mid-sixties, with thick tortoiseshell eyeglasses, a linen suit, and a mane of white hair that gave him a learned air. His scholarly demeanor swiftly evaporated. Only Elwood was dismayed by the teacher's distracted, lackluster efforts; the other boys spent the morning goofing and joshing. Griff and his cronies played spades at the back of the classroom, and when Elwood caught Turner's eye, the boy was reading a wrinkled Superman comic. Turner saw him, shrugged, and turned the page. Desmond was out cold, his neck cracked at a painful angle.

Elwood, who did all of Mr. Marconi's accounting in his head, took the rudimentary math lesson as an insult. He was supposed to be taking college classes—that's why he was in that car in the first place. He shared a primer with the boy next to him, a fat kid who burped up breakfast in powerful gusts, and they started a dumb game of tug-of-war. Most of the Nickel boys couldn't read. As each boy picked up that morning's story—nonsense about an industrious hare—Mr. Goodall didn't bother to correct them or share the proper pronunciation. Elwood carved each syllable with such precision that the students around him stirred from their reveries, curious as to what kind of black boy talked like that.

He approached Goodall at the lunch bell and the teacher pretended to know him: "Hello, son, what can I do for you?" Another one of his colored boys, they came and went. Up close, Goodall's pink cheeks and nose were lumpy and riddled. His sweat, accented by last night's bottle, was a sweet vapor.

Elwood kept the indignation out of his voice when he asked if Nickel had advanced classes for students who were looking forward to college. He'd learned this material years ago, he explained humbly.

Goodall was amiable enough. "Certainly! I'll speak to the director about it. What was your name again?"

Elwood caught up with Desmond on the path back to Cleveland. He told Desmond about his conversation with the teacher. Desmond said, "You believe that shit?"

After lunch, when it was time for art class and shop, Blakeley pulled Elwood aside. The house father wanted Elwood to work on the yard crew with some of the Grubs. He'd be joining the other boys in the middle of their shift, but grounds work gave you the lay of the land, so to speak. "See it close up," Blakeley said.

That first afternoon, Elwood and five other boys—most of them chucks—prowled over the colored half of campus with scythes and rakes. Their leader was a quiet-natured boy named Jaimie, who had the spindly, undernourished frame common to Nickel students. He bounced around Nickel a lot—his mother was Mexican, so they didn't know what to do with him. On his arrival, he was put in with the white kids, but his first day working in the lime fields he got so dark that Spencer had him reassigned to the colored half. Jaimie spent a month in Cleveland, but then Director Hardee toured one day, took a look at that light face among the dark faces, and had him sent back to the white camp. Spencer bided his time and tossed him back a few weeks later. "I go back and forth," Jaimie said as he raked up pine needles into a mound. He had the screwed-down smile of the rickety-toothed. "One day they'll make up their minds, I suppose."

Elwood got his tour as they cut their way up the hill, past the two other colored dormitories, the red clay basketball courts, and the big laundry building. Looking down, most of the white campus was visible through the trees: the three dormitories, the hospital, and administration buildings. The head of the school, Director Hardee, worked in the big red one with the American flag. There were the big facilities the black boys and white boys used at different times, like the gymnasium, the chapel, and the woodshop.

From above, the white schoolhouse was identical to the colored one. Elwood wondered if it was in better shape, like the schools in Tallahassee, or if Nickel delivered the same stunted education to all its charges regardless of skin color.

When they got to the top of the hill, the yard crew turned around. On the other side of the rise was the graveyard, Boot Hill. A low wall of rough stones enclosed the white crosses, gray weeds, the bent and lurching trees. The boys gave it a wide berth.

If you took the road past the other side of the slope, Jaimie explained, eventually you reached the printing plant, the first set of farms, and then the swamp that marked the northern end of the property. "You'll be picking potatoes sooner or later, don't worry," he told Elwood. Gangs of students walked the trails and roads to their work assignments while supervisors in their state cars crisscrossed the property, watching. Elwood stood in wonder at the sight of a black boy, thirteen or fourteen years old, driving an old tractor that pulled a wooden trailer full of students. The driver looked sleepy and serene in his big seat, taking his charges to the farm.

When the other boys stiffened and stopped talking, it meant that Spencer was about.

Midway between the colored and the white campuses stood a single-story rectangular building, short and skinny, that Elwood took for a storage shed. Rust stains fell like vines across the white paint covering its concrete-block walls, but the green trim around the windows and front door was fresh and bright. The longer wall had one big window with three smaller ones next to it like ducklings.

A patch of uncut grass, a foot wide, encircled the building, untouched and untamed. "Should we cut that, too?" Elwood asked.

The two boys next to Elwood sucked their teeth. "Nigger, you don't go that way unless they take you," one said.

Elwood spent his free time before supper in Cleveland's rec room. He explored the cabinets, where they kept the cards and games and spiders. Students argued over who was next for table tennis, slapped paddles toward the saggy net, and cursed over wild shots, the pop of the white balls like the ragged heartbeat of an adolescent afternoon. Elwood checked out the meager offerings on the bookshelves, the Hardy Boys and comic books. There were moldy volumes about the natural sciences with space vistas and close-ups of the seafloor. He opened one cardboard chess set. There were only three pieces inside—a rook and two pawns.

The other students circulated, to or from work or sports, upstairs to the bunks, into their private recesses of mischief. Mr. Blakeley stopped on his way through and introduced Elwood to Carter, one of the black housemen. He was younger than the house father and carried himself like a stickler. Carter gave him a quick, dubious nod and turned to tell a thumb-sucker in the corner to knock it off.

Half of the housemen in Cleveland were black and half were white. "You got a coin toss over whether they look the other way or hassle you," Desmond said, "no matter what color they are." Desmond lay on one of the couches, his head on the funny pages to prevent it from touching an unwholesome stain on the upholstery. "Most are okay, but some of them got that mad-dog shit in them." Desmond pointed out the student captain, whose job it was to keep track of infractions and attendance. This week Cleveland's captain was a light-skinned boy with thick gold curls named Birdy—he was pigeon-toed. Birdy patrolled the first floor with the clipboard and pencil that were the trappings of his office, humming happily. "This one will rat on you in a second," Desmond said, "but get a good captain and you can scrape up some nice merits for Explorer or Pioneer."

An air horn screeched to the south, down the hill. No telling what it was. Elwood turned over a wooden crate and slumped down. Where to fit this place into the path of his life? The paint hung in thin rinds from the ceiling, and the sooty windows turned every hour overcast. He was thinking of Dr. King's speech to high school students in Washington, DC, when he spoke of the degradations of Jim Crow and the need to transform that degradation into action. *It will enrich your spirit as nothing else can. It will give you that rare sense of nobility that can only spring from love and selflessly helping your fellow man. Make a career of humanity. Make it a central part of your life.*

I am stuck here, but I'll make the best of it, Elwood told himself, and I'll make it brief. Everybody back home knew him as even, dependable—Nickel would soon understand that about him, too. At dinner, he'd ask Desmond how many points he needed to move out of Grub, how long it took most people to advance and graduate. Then he'd do it twice as fast. This was his resistance.

With that, he went through three chess sets, made a complete set of pieces, and won two games in a row.

Why he intervened in the fight in the bathroom, he couldn't muster a proper answer later. It was something his grandfather might have done in one of Harriet's stories: stepped up when he saw something wrong.

The younger boy being bullied, Corey, was not someone he'd met before. The bullies he'd encountered at his breakfast table: Lonnie with his bulldog face, and his manic partner Black Mike. Elwood went into the first-floor bathroom to urinate, and the taller boys had Corey up against the cracked tile wall. Maybe it was because Elwood didn't have any goddamned sense, as the Frenchtown boys said. Maybe it was because they were bigger and the other guy was smaller. His lawyer had persuaded the judge to let Elwood spend his last free days at home; there was no one to take him to Nickel that day, and the Tallahassee jail was overcrowded. Perhaps if he'd spent more time in the crucible of the county jail, Elwood would have known that it is best not to interfere in other people's violence, no matter the underlying facts of the incident.

Elwood said, "Hey," and took a step forward. Black Mike spun around, slugged him in the jaw and knocked him back against the sink.

Another boy, a chuck, opened the bathroom door and yelled, "Oh, shit." Phil, one of the white housemen, was making the rounds. He had a drowsy way about him and usually pretended not to see what was right in front of his face. At a young age he had decided it was easier that way. A coin toss, as Desmond had described Nickel justice. This day Phil said, "What are you little niggers up to?" His tone was light, more curious than anything else. Interpreting the scene was not part of his job. Who was at fault, who started it, why. His job was to keep these colored boys in check and today his responsibilities were not outside his grasp. He knew the names of the other boys. He asked the new boy his name.

"Mr. Spencer will take this up," Phil said. He told the boys to get ready for dinner.

CHAPTER SIX

The white boys bruised differently than the black boys and called it the Ice Cream Factory because you came out with bruises of every color. The black boys called it the White House because that was its official name and it fit and didn't need to be embellished. The White House delivered the law and everybody obeyed.

They came at one a.m. but woke few, because it was hard to sleep when you knew they were coming, even if they weren't coming for you. The boys heard the cars grind gravel outside, the doors open, the thumping up the stairs. The hearing was seeing, too, in bright strokes across the mind's canvas. The men's flashlights danced. They knew where their beds were—the bunks were only two feet apart, and after occasions when they grabbed the wrong ones, now they made sure beforehand. They took Lonnie and Big Mike, they took Corey, and they got Elwood, too.

The night visitors were Spencer and a houseman named Earl, who was big and quick, which helped when a boy broke down in one of the back rooms and had to be put back on course so they could proceed. The state cars were brown Chevys, the ones that roved the grounds all day on simple errands but at night became harbingers. Spencer driving

Lonnie and Black Mike and Earl taking Elwood and Corey, who had been weeping all night.

No one talked to Elwood at dinner, as if what was coming was catching. Some boys whispered when he passed—*What a dummy*—and the bullies gave him angry looks, but mostly there was a heavy pressure of menace and unease in the dormitory that didn't end until they took the boys away. The rest of the boys relaxed then and some were even able to dream.

At lights-out, Desmond whispered to Elwood that once it started, it was best not to move. The strap had a notch cut into it, and it'd snag on you and slice if you were not still. In the car over, Corey made an incantation, "I'm-a hold on and be still, I'm-a hold on and be still," so maybe it was true. Elwood didn't ask how many times Desmond had gone down because the boy stopped talking after that piece of advice.

The White House, in its previous use, had been a work shed. They parked behind it and Spencer and his man took them in through the back. The beating entrance, the boys called it. Passing by the road out front, you'd never look twice. Spencer quickly found the key on his enormous key ring and opened the two padlocks. The stench was fierce—urine and other things that had soaked into the concrete. A single naked bulb buzzed in the hallway. Spencer and Earl led them past the two cells to the room at the front of the building, where a line of bolted-together chairs waited, and a table.

Right there was the front door. Elwood thought of running. He didn't. This place was why the school had no wall or fence or barbed wire around it, why so few boys ran: It was the wall that kept them in.

Spencer and Earl took Black Mike in first. Spencer said, "Thought you'd be done after last time."

Earl said, "Piss himself again."

The roar began: an even gale. Elwood's chair vibrated with energy. He couldn't figure out what it was—some sort of machine—but it was loud enough to cover Black Mike's screams and the smack of the strap on his body. Halfway through, Elwood started counting, on the theory that if he knew how much the other boys got, he'd know how much he'd get. Unless there was a higher system to how many each boy got: repeat offender, instigator, bystander. No one had asked Elwood for his side of the story, that he was trying to break up the fight in the bathroom—but maybe he'd get less for stepping in. He counted up to twenty-eight before the beating stopped and they dragged Black Mike out to one of the cars.

Corey continued to sob, and when Spencer came back he told him to shut his fucking mouth and they took Lonnie in for his. Lonnie got around sixty. It was impossible to make out what Spencer and Earl said to him back there, but Lonnie needed more instructions or admonishments than his partner.

They took Corey in for his and Elwood noticed there was a Bible on the table.

Corey got around seventy—Elwood lost his place a few times—and it didn't make sense, why did the bullies get less than the bullied? Now he had no idea what he was in for. It didn't make sense. Maybe they lost count, too. Maybe there was no system at all to the violence and no one, not the keepers nor the kept, knew what happened or why.

Then it was Elwood's time. The two cells faced each

other, separated by the hallway. The beating room had a bloody mattress and a naked pillow that was covered instead by the overlapping stains from all the mouths that had bit into it. Also: the gigantic industrial fan that was the source of the roaring, the sound that traveled all over campus, farther than physics allowed. Its original home was the laundry—in the summer those old machines made an inferno—but after one of the periodic reforms where the state made up new rules about corporal punishment, someone had the bright idea to bring it in here. Splatter on the walls where the fan had whipped up blood in its gusting. There was a weird thing to the acoustics where the fan covered the boys' screams but right next to it you heard the staff's instructions perfectly: *Hold on to the rail and don't let go. Make a sound and you'll get more. Shut your fucking mouth, nigger.*

The strap was three feet long with a wooden handle, and they had called it Black Beauty since before Spencer's time, although the one he held in his hand was not the original: She had to be repaired or replaced every so often. The leather slapped across the ceiling before it came down on your legs, to tell you it was about to come down, and the bunk springs made noise with each blow. Elwood held on to the top of the bed and bit into the pillow but he passed out before they were done, so when people asked later how many licks he got, he didn't know.

CHAPTER SEVEN

Rarely did Harriet make proper goodbyes to her loved ones. Her father died in jail after a white lady downtown accused him of not getting out of her way on the sidewalk. *Bumptious contact*, as Jim Crow defined it. That's how it went in the old days. He was waiting for his appointment with the judge when they found him hung in his cell. No one believed the police's story. "Niggers and jail," her uncle said, "niggers and jail." Two days prior, Harriet had waved to him across the street on her way home from school. That was her last image of him: Her big, cheerful daddy walking to his second job.

Harriet's husband, Monty, got hit in the head with a chair while breaking up a scuffle at Miss Simone's. Some colored GIs from Camp Gordon Johnston in a rumble with a bunch of Tallahassee crackers over who had next on the pool table. Two people ended up dead. One of them was her Monty, who'd stepped up to protect one of Simone's dishwashers from three white men. The boy still wrote Harriet letters every Christmas. He drove a taxicab in Orlando and had three kids.

She said goodbye to her daughter, Evelyn, and her son-in-law, Percy, the night they took off. Percy's was one leave-taking in the works for years, although she hadn't foreseen that he'd take Evelyn. Percy had been too big for the town since he got back from the war. He served in the Pacific theater, behind the lines keeping up the supply chain.

He came back evil. Not because of what happened overseas but from what he saw on his return. He loved the army, and even received a commendation for a letter he wrote to his captain about inequities in the treatment of colored soldiers. Perhaps his life might have veered elsewhere if the US government had opened the country to colored advancement like they opened the army. But it was one thing to allow someone to kill for you and another to let him live next door. The GI Bill fixed things pretty good for the white boys he served with, but the uniform meant different things depending who wore it. What was the point of a no-interest loan when a white bank won't let you step inside? Percy drove up to Milledgeville to visit a buddy from his unit and some crackers started something. He'd stopped for gas in one of those little towns. Cracker town, crack-your-head town. He barely got out—everybody knew white boys were lynching black men in uniform, but he never believed he'd be a target. Not him. Bunch of white boys jealous that they didn't have a uniform and afraid of a world that let a nigger wear one in the first place.

Evelyn married him. She was always going to, since they were small. Elwood's arrival did nothing to still Percy's wildness: the corn whiskey and roadhouse nights, the roguish element he brought into their house on Brevard Street. Evelyn had never been very strong; when Percy was around she shrank to an appendage of his, an extra arm or a leg. A mouth: He had Evelyn tell Harriet that they were leaving for California to try their luck.

"What kind of people leave for California in the middle of the night?" Harriet asked.

"I got to meet someone about an opportunity," Percy said.

Harriet thought they should wake the boy. "Let him sleep," Evelyn said, and that was the last she heard from them. If her daughter had ever been suited for motherhood, she never demonstrated it. The look on her face when little Elwood suckled on her breast—her joyless, empty eyes seeing through the walls of the house and into pure nothing—chilled Harriet to the bone whenever she remembered it.

The day the court officer came for Elwood was the worst goodbye. It had been the two of them for so long. She and Mr. Marconi would make sure the lawyer kept on fixing his case, she said. Mr. Andrews was from Atlanta, a brand of young white crusader who went north to get his law degree and came back changed. Harriet never let him go without a bite to eat. He was extravagant with his praise for her cobbler and in his optimism over Elwood's prospects.

They'd find a way out of this mess of thorns, she told her grandson, and promised to visit his first Sunday at Nickel. But when she showed up, they told her that he was sick and couldn't have visitors.

She asked what was wrong with him. The Nickel man said, "How the hell should I know, lady?"

There was a new pair of denim pants on the chair next to Elwood's hospital bed. The beating had embedded bits of the first into his skin and it took two hours for the doctor to remove the fibers. It was a duty the doctor had to perform from time to time. Tweezers did the trick. The boy would be in the hospital until he walked without pain.

Dr. Cooke had an office next to the examination rooms,

where he smoked cigars and harangued his wife on the telephone all day, bickering over money or her no-account relatives. The potato-y cigar smoke permeated the ward, covering the smell of sweat and vomit and gamey skin, and dissipated by dawn, when he'd show up and perfume the place again. There was a glass case full of bottles and boxes of medicine that he unlocked with great seriousness, but he only ever reached for the big bucket of aspirin.

Elwood spent his stay on his stomach. For obvious reasons. The hospital inducted him into its rhythms. Nurse Wilma grunted around most days, hale and brusque, slamming drawers and cabinets. She kept her hair in a licorice-red bouffant and dotted her cheeks with rouge so that she reminded Elwood of a haunted doll come to hideous life, something out of horror comics. *The Crypt of Terror*, *The Vault of Horror*, read by window light in his cousin's attic. Horror comics, he'd noticed, delivered two kinds of punishment—completely undeserved, and sinister justice for the wicked. He placed his current misfortune in the former category and waited to turn the page.

Nurse Wilma was almost sweet to the white boys who came in with their abrasions and ailments, a second mother. Nary a kind word for the black boys. Elwood's bedpan was a particular affront—she looked as if he'd pissed in her outstretched palms. More than once in his protest dreams, hers was the face of the waitress behind the counter who refused to serve him, the housewife with the spit-flecked mouth cursing like a sailor. That he dreamed of a time when he was outside and marching kept his spirits up each morning when he woke in the hospital. His mind still capable of travel.

That first day there was only one other boy in the hospital, his bed hidden behind a folding curtain at the far end of the ward. When Nurse Wilma or Dr. Cooke tended to him, they closed it behind them, the wheels of the curtain squeaking across the white tile. The patient never spoke when the staff addressed him, but their voices had a cheerful quality that was absent when they talked to the other boys: The kid was a terminal case, or royalty. None of the students who stayed on the ward knew who he was or what landed him there.

The cast of boys came in and out. Elwood got to know some white kids he wouldn't have met otherwise. Wards of the state, orphans, runaways who'd lit out to get away from mothers who entertained men for money or to escape rummy fathers who came into their rooms in the middle of the night. Some of them were rough characters. They stole money, cussed at their teachers, damaged public property, had stories about bloody pool-hall fights and uncles who sold moonshine. They were sent to Nickel for offenses Elwood had never heard of: malingering, mopery, incorrigibility. Words the boys didn't understand either, but what was the point when their meaning was clear enough: Nickel. *I got busted for sleeping in a garage to keep warm, I stole five dollars from my teacher, I drank a bottle of cough syrup and went wild one night. I was on my own trying to get by.*

"Wow, they got you good," Dr. Cooke said whenever he changed Elwood's dressings. Elwood didn't want to look but he had to. He got a glimpse of his inner thighs, where the raw slashes on the backs of his legs crept up like gruesome fingers. Dr. Cooke gave him an aspirin and retreated to his office. Five minutes later he was arguing with his wife over a shiftless cousin who needed a loan for a scheme.

Some snuffling dude woke Elwood in the middle of the night and he was up for hours, his skin burning and wriggling under the bandages.

A week into his hospital stay, he opened his eyes and Turner lay in the bed opposite. Whistling the theme to *The Andy Griffith Show,* cheerful and fluttering. He was a good whistler and for the remainder of their friendship his performances provided a score, capturing the mood of the escapade or fluting a countervailing commentary.

Turner waited until Nurse Wilma went outside for a cigarette and explained his visit. "Thought I'd take me a vacation," he said. He'd eaten some soap powder to make himself sick, an hour of stomachache for a whole day off. Or two—he knew how to sell it. "Got some more powder hidden in my sock, too," he said. Elwood turned away to brood.

"How you like that witch doctor?" Turner asked later. Dr. Cooke had just taken the temperature of a white boy down the row who was puffed up and moaning like a cow. The phone rang, the doctor dropped two aspirin into the white kid's palm and hoofed it to his office.

Turner rolled up to Elwood. He was clackety-clacking around the ward in one of the old polio wheelchairs. He said, "Come in here with your damn head cut off and he'd give you aspirin."

Elwood didn't want to chuckle, like it would be cheating on his pain, but he couldn't help it. His testicles were swole up from where the strap landed between his legs, and his laughter tugged something inside and made them hurt again.

"Nigger come in here," Turner said, "head cut off, both legs, both arms cut off, and that fucking witch doctor would be like, 'You want one tablet, or two?' " He coaxed the stuck wheels of the wheelchair and huffed away.

There was nothing to read apart from *The Gator*, the school newspaper, and a pamphlet commemorating the school's fiftieth anniversary, both printed on the other side of campus by Nickel students. Every boy in every picture was smiling, but even after Elwood's short stay he recognized a kind of Nickel deadness in their eyes. He suspected he had it, too, now that he had fully enrolled. Turning slowly on his side, propped on an elbow, he went through the pamphlet a few times.

The state opened the school in 1899 as the Florida Industrial School for Boys. "A reform school where the young offender of law, separated from vicious associates, may receive physical, intellectual, and moral training, be reformed and restored to the community with purpose and character fitting for a good citizen, an honorable and an honest man with a trade or skilled occupation fitting such person for self-maintenance." The boys were called students, rather than inmates, to distinguish them from the violent offenders that populated prisons. All the violent offenders, Elwood added, were on staff.

When it opened, the school admitted children as young as five, a fact that swept up Elwood in a lament when he tried to sleep: all those helpless kids. The first thousand acres were granted by the state; over the years locals generously donated another four hundred. Nickel earned its keep. The construction of the printing plant was a bona fide success by any measure. "In 1926 alone, publishing created a profit of $250,000, in addition to introducing the students to a useful trade in which to apply themselves after graduation." The brick-making machine produced twenty thousand bricks a day; its issue propped up buildings all over Jackson County, big and small. The school's annual Christmas-light display, designed and executed by the students, drew visitors from miles around. Every year the newspaper sent out a reporter.

In 1949, the year of the pamphlet's publication, the school was renamed in honor of Trevor Nickel, a reformer who'd taken over a few years earlier. The boys used to say it was because their lives weren't worth five cents, but it was not the case. Occasionally you passed Trevor Nickel's portrait in the hallway and he frowned like he knew what you were thinking. No, that wasn't it: Like he knew you knew what he was thinking.

The next time one of the ringworm boys came in from Cleveland, Elwood asked the kid to bring back some books for him to read, and he did. Plopped down a stack of battered natural-science books that by accident provided a course in ancient forces: tectonic collisions, mountain ranges thrown up to the sky, volcanic bombast. All the violence roiling beneath that makes the world above. They were big books with exuberant pictures, red and orange, in contrast with the cloudy, white-gone-gray of the ward.

Turner's second day in the hospital, Elwood caught him pulling a piece of folded cardboard out of his sock. Turner swallowed the contents and an hour later he was hollering. Dr. Cooke came out and he threw up on the man's shoes.

"I told you not to eat the food," Dr. Cooke said. "It's going to make you sick, what they serve here."

"What else am I supposed to eat, Mr. Cooke?"

The doctor blinked.

When Turner finished mopping up the vomit, Elwood said, "Doesn't that hurt your stomach?"

"Sure it does, man," Turner said. "But I don't feel like

going to work today. These beds are lumpy as hell, but you can get some good shut-eye, you figure out how to lay on them."

The secret boy behind the folded curtain made a heavy sigh, and Elwood and Turner jumped. He didn't make much noise as a rule and you forgot he was around.

"Hey!" Elwood said. "You over there!"

"Shhh!" went Turner.

There was no sound, not even the shifting of a blanket.

"You go look," Elwood said. Something had settled—he felt better today. "See who it is. Ask what's wrong with him."

Turner looked at him like he was nuts. "I ain't asking nobody shit."

"Scared?" Elwood said, like one of the boys from his street, how buddies taunted each other back home.

"Damn," Turner said, "you don't know. Pop back there for a look, maybe you have to trade places with him. Like in a ghost story."

That night Nurse Wilma stayed late, reading to the kid behind the curtain. The Bible, a hymn, it sounded how people sound when they have God in their mouth.

The beds were occupied and then they weren't. A bad batch of canned peaches filled the ward. There weren't enough beds so they slept head to toe, gassy and gurgling. The beds turned over. Grubs, Explorers, and the industrious Pioneers. Injured, infected, faking it, and afflicted. Spider bite, busted ankle, lost a fingertip in a loading machine. A visit to the White House. Knowing that he'd gone down, the other boys no longer kept him at a distance. He was one of them now.

Elwood got sick of looking at his new pants sitting there on the chair. He folded them up and stuffed them under his mattress.

The big radio over by Dr. Cooke's office played all day, competing with the noise of the metal shop next door—electric saws, steel on steel. The doctor thought the radio was therapeutic; Nurse Wilma saw no reason to coddle the boys. *Don McNeill's Breakfast Club*, preachers and serials, the soaps Elwood's grandmother listened to. The problems of the white people in radio shows had been remote, belonging to another country. Now they were a ride home to Frenchtown.

Elwood hadn't heard *Amos 'n' Andy* in years. His grandmother turned off the radio when *Amos 'n' Andy* came on, with its carousel of malapropisms and demeaning misadventures. "White people like that stuff, but we don't have to listen to it." She was glad when she read in the *Defender* that it had been taken off the air. A station around Nickel broadcast old episodes, haunted transmissions. No one touched the dial when the old reruns came on and everyone laughed at Amos and Kingfish's antics, black boys and white boys alike. "Holy mackerel!"

One of the radio stations sometimes played the theme to *The Andy Griffith Show*, and Turner whistled in accompaniment.

"Aren't you worried they'll know you're faking it," Elwood said. "Whistling happy like that?"

"I ain't faking—that soap powder is awful," Turner said. "But it's me choosing, not anyone else."

That was a dumb way of looking at it, but Elwood didn't say anything. The theme music was stuck in his head now, and Elwood would have hummed or whistled but he didn't want to look like a copycat. The song was a tiny, quiet piece of America carved out of the rest. No fire hoses, no need for the National Guard. It occurred to Elwood that he'd never seen a Negro in the small town of Mayberry, where the show took place.

A man on the radio announced that Sonny Liston was going to fight an up-and-comer named Cassius Clay. "Who's that?" Elwood said.

"Some nigger about to get knocked down," Turner said.

One afternoon Elwood was half dozing when the noise paralyzed him—the keys like a wind chime. Spencer was on the ward to see the doctor. Elwood waited for the sound of the leather strap scraping the ceiling before it came down . . . Then the superintendent was gone and the sound of the radio commanded the room again. He sweat through to his sheets.

"Do they do it like that to everybody?" Elwood asked Turner after lunch. Nurse Wilma had distributed ham sandwiches and watery grape juice, white kids first.

Out of the blue, but Turner knew what Elwood was referring to. He rolled over in the polio chair, lunch in his lap. "Not like what you got," he said. "Not that bad. I've never gone down. I got smacked across the face for smoking once."

"I have a lawyer," Elwood said. "He can do something."

"You already got off lucky," Turner said.

"How come?"

Turner finished his juice with a slurp. "Sometimes they take you to the White House and we never see your ass again."

It was quiet on the ward except for them and the buzz

saw next door, keening. Elwood didn't want to know but he asked anyway.

"Your family asks the school what happened and they say you ran away," Turner said. He made sure the white boys weren't looking. "Problem was, Elwood," he said, "you didn't know how it works. Take Corey and those two cats. You wanted to do some Lone Ranger shit—run up and save a nigger. But they punked him out a long time ago. See, those three do that all the time. Corey likes it. They play rough, then he takes them into the stall or whatever and gets on his knees. That's how they do."

"I saw his face, he was scared," Elwood said.

"You don't know what makes him tick," Turner said. "You don't know what makes anybody tick. I used to think out there is out there and then once you're in here, you're in here. That everybody in Nickel was different because of what being here does to you. Spencer and them, too—maybe out there in the free world, they're good people. Smiling. Nice to their kids." His mouth squinched up, like he was sucking on a rotten tooth. "But now that I been out and I been brought back, I know there's nothing in here that changes people. In here and out there are the same, but in here no one has to act fake anymore."

He was talking in circles, everything pointing back at itself. Elwood said, "It's against the law." State law, but also Elwood's. If everyone looked the other way, then everybody was in on it. If he looked the other way, he was as implicated as the rest. That's how he saw it, how he'd always seen things.

Turner didn't say anything.

"It's not how it's supposed to be," Elwood said.

"Don't nobody care about supposed-to. If you call out Black Mike and Lonnie, you calling out everyone who lets it happen, too. You ratting on everybody."

"That's what I'm telling you." Elwood told Turner about his grandmother and the lawyer, Mr. Andrews. They'd report Spencer and Earl and anybody else up to no good. His teacher Mr. Hill was an activist. He'd marched all over—he hadn't returned to Lincoln High School after the summer because he was back organizing. Elwood wrote him about his arrest but wasn't sure if he got the letter. Mr. Hill knew people who'd want to know about a place like Nickel, once they got ahold of him. "It's not like the old days," Elwood said. "We can stand up for ourselves."

"That shit barely works out there—what do you think it's going to do in here?"

"You say that because there's no one else out there sticking up for you."

"That's true," Turner said. "That doesn't mean I can't see how it works. Maybe I see things more clearly because of it." He made a face as the soap powder gave him a kick. "The key to in here is the same as surviving out there—you got to see how people act, and then you got to figure out how to get around them like an obstacle course. If you want to walk out of here."

"Graduate."

"Walk out of here," Turner corrected. "You think you can do that? Watch and think? Nobody else is going to get you out—just you."

Dr. Cooke gave Turner the boot the next morning with two aspirin and a repeat of his prescription that he not eat the food. It was only Elwood on the ward then. The curtain that had been around the nameless boy was in the corner, folded flat into itself. The bed was empty. He'd disappeared sometime in the night without waking anyone.

Elwood intended to follow Turner's advice, and he meant it, but that was before he saw his legs. That defeated him for a spell.

He spent another five days in the hospital, then it was back with the other Nickel boys. School and work. He was one of them now in many ways, including his embrace of silence. When his grandmother came to visit, he couldn't tell her what he saw when Dr. Cooke removed the dressings and he walked the cold tile to the bathroom. Elwood got a look at himself then and knew that her heart wouldn't be able to take it, plus his shame in letting it happen. He was as far away from her as the others in her family who'd vanished and he was sitting right in front of her. On visiting day, he told her he was okay but sad, it was difficult but he was hanging in there, when all he wanted to say was, *Look at what they did to me, look at what they did to me.*

CHAPTER EIGHT

When Elwood got out he returned to the yard crew. Jaimie the Mexican had been chucked to the white side again so another boy was in charge. More than once Elwood caught himself swinging the scythe with too much violence, like he was attacking the grass with a leather strap. He'd stop and tell his heart to slow down. Ten days later, Jaimie was back with the colored boys—Spencer rooted him out—but he didn't mind. "That's my life, ping-pong."

Elwood's schooling was not going to improve. He had to accept that. He touched Mr. Goodall's arm outside the schoolhouse; the teacher didn't recognize him. Goodall repeated his promise to find more challenging work, but Elwood was onto the teacher now and didn't ask again. One late-November afternoon they sent Elwood with a team to clean out the basement of the schoolhouse, and he found a set of Chipwick's British Classics underneath some boxes containing calendars for 1954. Trollope and Dickens and people with names like that. Elwood went through the books one by one during school hours while the boys around him stuttered and stumbled. He had intended to study British literature at the college. Now he had to teach himself. It would have to do.

Punishment for acting above your station was a central principle in Harriet's interpretation of the world. In the hospital, Elwood wondered if the viciousness of his beating owed something to his request for harder classes: *Get that uppity nigger.* Now he worked on a new theory: There was no higher system guiding Nickel's brutality, merely an indiscriminate spite, one that had nothing to do with people. A figment from tenth-grade science struck him: a Perpetual Misery Machine, one that operated by itself without human agency. Also, Archimedes, one of his first encyclopedia finds. Violence is the only lever big enough to move the world.

He canvassed but didn't get a clear picture of how to graduate early. Desmond, that scientist of demerit and credit, was no help. "You get merits for behavior every week if you do what you're supposed to do, right off the bat. But if your house father mixes you up with someone else, or he's out to get you—zip. For demerits, you never know." The demerit scale varied from dormitory to dormitory. Smoking, fighting, perpetuating a state of dishevelment—the penalty depended on where they'd sent you and the whims of the local housemen. Blaspheming cost a hundred demerits in Cleveland—Blakeley was the God-fearing sort—but only fifty in Roosevelt. Jacking off was a flat two hundred demerits in Lincoln, but if you were caught jacking someone else off, it was only a hundred.

"Only a hundred?"

"That's Lincoln for you," Desmond said, as if explaining a foreign land, jinns and ducats.

Blakeley liked his hooch, Elwood noticed. The man was half-mast until noon. Did that mean he couldn't rely on the house father's accounts? Say he stayed out of trouble, Elwood asked, did everything right—how fast could he climb from the lowest level of Grub to the highest level of Ace? "If everything went perfect?"

"It's too late for perfect if you already went down," Desmond told him.

Problem was, even if you avoided trouble, trouble might reach out and snatch you anyway. Another student might sniff out a weakness and start something, one of the staff dislikes your smile and knocks it off your face. You might stumble into a bramble of bad luck of the sort that got you here in the first place. Elwood decided: By June he'd climb the merit ladder out of this pit, four months short of what that judge gave him. It was comforting—he was accustomed to measuring time according to the school calendar, so a June graduation made his Nickel term into a lost year. This time next fall, he'd be back at Lincoln High School for his senior year, and with Mr. Hill's endorsement, enrolled at Melvin Griggs again. They spent his college money on the lawyer, but if Elwood worked extra next summer, he'd make it back.

He had a date, now he needed a course of action. He felt rotten those first days out of the hospital until he came up with a scheme that combined Turner's advice with what he'd learned from his heroes in the movement. Watch and think and plan. Let the world be a mob—Elwood will walk through it. They might curse and spit and strike him, but he'd make it through to the other side. Bloodied and tired, but he'd make it through.

He waited, but no payback came from Lonnie and Black Mike. Except for an incident where Griff hip-checked

Elwood and sent him crashing down the stairs, they ignored him. Corey, the boy he'd stepped up to defend, winked at him once. Everyone had moved on to girding themselves for the next Nickel mishap, the one that was out of their hands.

One Wednesday after breakfast, Carter the houseman ordered Elwood over to the warehouse for a new detail. Turner was there, along with a young white man, a lanky sort with a beatnik slouch and a greasy spray of blond hair. Elwood had seen him around, smoking in the shade of various buildings. His name was Harper and according to staff records, he worked in Community Service. Harper looked Elwood over and said, "He'll do." The supervisor closed the big sliding door to the warehouse, bolted it, and they climbed into the front seat of a gray van. Unlike the other school vehicles, it didn't have Nickel's name painted on it.

Elwood sat in the middle. "Here we go," Turner said. He rolled down the window. "Harper asked who I thought should replace Smitty, and I said, you. I told him you weren't another one of these dummies they got around here."

Smitty was an older boy from Roosevelt dormitory next door. He'd hit the highest rank of Ace and graduated the week prior, although Elwood thought *graduate* was a moronic word to use. The boy couldn't read a lick, plain as day.

Harper said, "He said you can keep your mouth shut, which is a requirement." With that, they were off the grounds.

Since the hospital, Elwood and Turner hung out most days, killed afternoons in the Cleveland rec room playing checkers and Ping-Pong with Desmond and some of the other even-tempered boys. Turner usually stumbled into a room as if searching for something, then started bullshitting and forgot whatever errand had brought him there. He was better at chess than Elwood, told better jokes than Desmond, and unlike Jaimie, ran on a more consistent schedule. Elwood knew Turner was assigned to Community Service, but he got cagey when Elwood pressed further: "It's taking things and making sure they end up where they're supposed to end up in the end."

"What the f-f-fuck does that mean," Jaimie said. The boy was not a natural cusser, and his occasional stutter diminished the effect, but of the available vices at Nickel, he had adopted foul language as one of the tamer choices.

"It means Community Service," Elwood said.

The immediate meaning of Community Service was it allowed Elwood to pretend he'd never hitchhiked to college—for a few hours, he was out of Nickel. His first trip out in the free world since his arrival. Free world was prison slang, but it had migrated to the reformatory school because it made sense, transmitted through a boy who'd heard it from a hard-luck father or uncle, or from a staff member revealing how he really felt about his charges, despite the school vocabulary Nickel liked to use for itself.

The air was cool in Elwood's lungs, and everything outside the window dazzled, renewed. "This or this," his eye doctor asked at checkups, a choice between two lenses of different power. Elwood never ceased to marvel how you could walk around and get used to seeing only a fraction of the world. Not knowing you only saw a sliver of the real thing. *This or this?* Definitely *this*, all that the van tumbled past, the sudden majesty of everything, even the falling-down shotgun shacks and sad concrete-block houses, the junker cars half in the weeds in someone's yard. He saw a rusty sign for Wild Cherry Hi-C and was more thirsty than he'd ever been in his life.

Harper noticed the shift in Elwood's posture. "He likes being out," the supervisor said, and he and Turner laughed. He turned on the radio. Elvis was singing. Harper slapped the steering wheel in time.

In temperament, Harper was an unlikely Nickel employee. "All right for a white man," in Turner's estimation. He practically grew up on the grounds, raised by his mother's sister, a secretary in the administration building. He spent untold afternoons on the grounds as a mascot to the white students and picked up odd work when he was old enough. Painted reindeer in the annual Christmas display ever since he could hold a brush. Now he was twenty years old and worked full-time. "My aunt says I'm a get-along type," he told the boys one shift while they idled outside the five-and-ten. "I suppose I am. I grew up around you boys, white and colored, and I know you're just like me, but you had some bad luck."

They made four stops around the town of Eleanor before the fire chief's house. First was JOHN DINER—a rusty outline attested to a fallen-off letter and an apostrophe. They parked down the alley and Elwood got a look at the van's cargo: cartons and crates of Nickel's kitchen stores. Cans of peas, industrial tins of peaches, applesauce, baked beans, gravy. A selection of this week's shipment from the state of Florida.

Harper lit a cigarette and put his ear to a transistor radio: game on today. Turner handed boxes of green beans and sacks of onions down to Elwood before they brought them into the back entrance of the restaurant kitchen.

"Don't forget the molasses," Harper said.

When they finished, the owner emerged—a porky redneck whose apron was a palimpsest of dark stains—and clapped Harper on the back. He handed Harper an envelope and asked about his family.

"You know Aunt Lucille," Harper said. "Supposed to stay off her feet and never stays put for anything."

The next two stops were also restaurants—a barbecue stand and a meat-and-three joint over the county line—and then they unloaded a store of canned vegetables at the Top Shop Grocery. Harper folded each envelope of cash in half, snapped a rubber band around it, and tossed it into the glove compartment before the next destination.

Turner let the work speak for itself. Harper wanted to be certain about Elwood's comfort with his new detail. "You don't look surprised," the young white man said.

"It has to end up somewhere," Elwood responded.

"How things are done. Spencer tells me where to go, and he kicks it up to Director Hardee." Harper fiddled the dial after more rock and roll: Elvis popped up again. He was everywhere. "It used to be worse in the old days," Harper said, "from what my aunt says. But the state cracked down and now we lay off the south-campus stuff." Meaning, they only sold the black students' supplies. "We had this good old boy who used to run Nickel, Roberts, who would've sold the air you breathe if he could've. Now that was a crook!"

"Beats cleaning the toilets," Turner said. "Beats cutting grass, if you ask me."

It was nice to be out, and Elwood said so. In the coming months, Elwood saw all of Eleanor, Florida, as their three-man crew made the rounds. He got to know the back of the short Main Street, as Harper parked by the service entrances. Sometimes they unloaded notebooks and pencils, sometimes medicine and bandages, but mostly it was food. Thanksgiving turkeys and Christmas hams disappeared into the hands of fry cooks, and the assistant principal of the elementary school opened a box of erasers and counted them one by one. Elwood wondered why the boys had no toothpaste—now he knew. They parked behind the five-and-ten, Fisher's Drugs, and phoned ahead to the local doctor, who slithered up to the driver's window with a furtive air. Once in a while they stopped at a green three-story house on a dead-end street and Harper got paid by a well-groomed city-council type in a sweater vest. Harper didn't know the guy's story, he said, but the man had good manners, crisp bills, and liked to talk Florida teams.

This or this? Every time he left school property, the new lens popped into place, and all it permitted him to see.

The first day, when the back of the van was empty, Elwood assumed they'd return to Nickel, but they headed to a clean, quiet street that reminded him of the nicer parts of Tallahassee, the white part. They pulled up at a big white house that floated on a sea of undulating green. An American flag sighed on a pole attached to the roof. They got out, and another look in the recesses of the van revealed a canvas tarp that hid painting supplies.

"Mrs. Davis," Harper said, bowing his head.

A white lady with a beehive hairdo waved from the front porch. "This is so exciting," she said.

Elwood didn't make eye contact as she led them around the back of the yard, where a gray, tired-looking gazebo perched at the edge of the oak trees.

"That it?" Harper asked.

"My grandfather built it forty years ago," Mrs. Davis said. "Conrad proposed to me right there." She wore a yellow dress with a houndstooth pattern and dark sunglasses like Jackie Kennedy. She spotted a thin green bug on her shoulder, flicked it off, and smiled.

A new paint job was in order. Mrs. Davis gave Harper a broom, Harper gave Elwood the broom, and Elwood swept the decking while Turner got the paint from the van.

"You boys are so nice to help us out here," Mrs. Davis told them before she returned to the house.

"I'll be back around three," Harper said. Then he was gone, too.

Turner explained that Harper had a girlfriend on Maple. Her man worked at one of the factories and kept long hours.

"We're going to paint?" Elwood said.

"Yeah, man."

"He's leaving us here?"

"Yeah, man. Mr. Davis is the fire chief. He has us out here a lot, doing little stuff. Smitty and I did all the rooms on the top floor." He pointed to the dormer windows as if it were possible for Elwood to appraise his handiwork. "All those guys on the school board, they have us do chores. Sometimes it's some bullshit, but I'll take being out here over any job back at school."

As did Elwood. It was a humid November afternoon and he savored the free-world sounds of bugs and birds. Their mating calls and warnings were soon accompanied by Turner's whistling—Chuck Berry, if Elwood was not mistaken. The brand of paint was Dixie, the color Dixie White.

The last time Elwood had done any painting, he'd given Mrs. Lamont's outhouse a new coat, a chore for which his grandmother had loaned him out for ten cents. Turner laughed and told Elwood how in the olden days, the school sent teams of boys into Eleanor all the time to do work for the big shots. According to Harper, sometimes it was favors, like this paint job, but a lot of time it was for real money, which schools kept for their "upkeep," same as the money from the crops, and the printing jobs, and the bricks. Further back, it was more gruesome. "When you graduated, you didn't go back to your family, you had parole where they basically sold your monkey ass to people in town. Work like a slave, live in their basement or whatever. Beat you, kick you, feed you shit."

"Shit food, like we get now?"

"Hell, no. Way worse." You had to work off your debt, he said. Then they let you go.

"Debt from what?"

That stumped him. "I never thought about it that way." He stayed Elwood's arm. "You don't want to go too fast," he said. "This can be a three-day job, we play it right. Mrs. Davis brings out lemonade."

When two glasses of lemonade appeared on a bronze tray, it was excellent.

They finished the railings and lattice of the walls. Elwood shook a new can of Dixie White, pried it open, and stirred. He'd told Turner how he got pinched and sent to Nickel—"Man, that's a raw deal"—but Turner never talked about his old life. This was his second term at the school after being out almost a year. Maybe asking about how he got snatched back was a way in. The Nickel undertow sucked up everything, and his friend's past might get pulled into the story.

Turner sat down at Elwood's question. "You know what a pinsetter is?"

"In a bowling alley," Elwood said.

"I was working as a pinsetter in a bowling alley down in Tampa, the Holiday. Most places, they got the machine that does it, but Mr. Garfield was hanging in there. He liked to see his pin boys crouch at the end of the lane like we were sprinters. Or dogs about to go out hunting. It wasn't a bad job. Picking up the pins after each throw and setting them up for the next frame. Mr. Garfield was a friend of the Everetts, where I was living. The state paid the Everetts money to take in kids. Some money, not a lot. There were always a lot of us strays around, coming and going.

"Like I said, it was a good job. Thursday was colored night, and everybody came from all around, the different colored bowling leagues, and that was a good time, but mostly it was these stupid rednecks from Tampa. Some bad, some less bad—white people. I was pretty fast and I find it easy to smile when I'm working, being somewhere else in my thoughts while I'm doing whatever, and the customers liked me, they gave me tips. I got to know some of the regulars. Not like know them, but we saw each other every week. Like that. I started goofing off with them—if it was a guy I knew, I might make a joke when they fouled, or make some clown face like this when they threw a gutter or had some funny-looking split. That became my routine, joking around with the regulars, and I liked the tips.

"There was this old head who worked in the kitchen, his name was Lou. One of those dudes you know have seen some shit. He didn't talk much to us pin boys, he flipped burgers. Because he wasn't too friendly, we didn't conversate much.

This one night I was on my break and I go out for a cigarette behind the grill. And he's there. In this apron, covered with grease. It was a hot night. And he looks me up and down. He says to me, 'I see you out there, nigger, putting on a show. Why you always shucking and jiving for these white people? Ain't nobody ever teach you self-respect?'

"Two other setters are out there and they hear this, they're like, *damn*. My face got all hot, I was ready to punch this old fool—he doesn't know me. Don't know shit about me. I look at him, and he ain't moving, standing there smoking this cigarette he rolled, and he knows I'm not going to do anything. Because he's right in what he said.

"Next time I was on a shift, I don't know, I started doing it differently. Instead of joking with them, I was mean. When they hit the gutter or stepped over the line, there was nothing friendly in my face. I saw in their eyes when they realized the game had changed. Maybe we'd pretended to be on the same side before and it was all equal, but now it wasn't.

"End of the night, I'd been taunting this fucking peckerwood the whole game. This big heehaw meathead. It's his turn and he has to pick up a 4–6 split. I said, 'Ain't that a stinker,' like Bugs Bunny, and that's it for him—he comes charging up the lane. He's chasing me around the place, I'm jumping from lane to lane, up in everybody's business, dodging balls, and then finally his friends hold him back. They come there all the time, they're not trying to make things hard for Mr. Garfield. They know me, or thought they knew me until I started not acting right, and they get their friend and cool him out and leave."

Turner grinned as he acted out the story. Until the last

part. He squinted at the floor of the gazebo as if trying to make out something tiny. "That was the end of it, really," he said, scratching the nick in his ear. "Next week I saw that guy's car in the parking lot and I threw a cinder block through the window and the cops picked me up."

Harper was an hour late. They weren't going to complain. Free time at Nickel on one side, work time in the free world on the other—it was an easy calculation. "Going to need a ladder," Elwood told Harper when he showed up.

"Sure," Harper said.

Mrs. Davis waved from the porch as they pulled away.

"How's your lady, Harper?" Turner asked.

Harper tucked in his shirttail. "Just when you ease into a good time, they bring up some whole other thing they been thinking about since the last time you saw them."

"Sure, I know," Turner said. He reached for Harper's cigarettes and lit one.

Elwood grabbed everything he saw in the free world to reassemble it in his mind later. What things looked like and what things smelled like and other things as well. Two days later Harper told him he was on Community Service permanently. But then, white men had always noticed his industrious nature. The news brightened his mood. Each time they returned to Nickel, he wrote down the particulars in a composition book. The date. The name of the individual and the establishment. Some names took a while to fill in, but Elwood had always been the patient type, and thorough.

CHAPTER NINE

The boys rooted for Griff even though he was a miserable bully who jimmied and pried at their weaknesses and made up weaknesses if he couldn't find any, such as calling you a "knock-kneed piece of shit" even if your knees had never knocked your whole life. He tripped them and laughed at the ensuing pratfalls and slapped them around when he could get away with it. He punked them out, dragging them into dark rooms. He smelled like a horse and made fun of their mothers, which was pretty low given the general motherlessness of the student population. He stole their desserts on multiple occasions—swiped from trays with a grin—and even if the desserts in question were no great shakes, it was the principle. The boys rooted for Griff because he was going to represent the colored half of Nickel at the annual boxing match, and no matter what he did the rest of the year, the day of the fight he was all of them in one black body and he was going to knock that white boy out.

If Griff spat teeth before that happened, swell.

The colored boys had held the Nickel title for fifteen years. Old hands on staff remembered the last white champion and still talked him up; other things from the old days they discussed less often. Terry "Doc" Burns was an anvil-handed good old boy from a musty corner of Suwannee County who'd been sent to Nickel for strangling a neighbor's chickens. Twenty-one chickens, to be exact, because "they were out to get him." Pain rolled off him like rain from a slate roof. After Doc Burns returned to the free world, the white boys who advanced to the final fight were pikers, so wobbly that over the years tall tales about the former champion grew more extravagant: Nature had gifted Doc Burns with an unnaturally long reach; he did not tire; his legendary combo swatted down every comer and rattled windows. In fact, Doc Burns had been beaten and ill-treated by so many in his life—family and stranger alike—that by the time he arrived at Nickel all punishments were gentle breezes.

This was Griff's first term on the boxing team. He arrived at Nickel in February, right after the graduation of the previous champ, Axel Parks. Axel should have graduated before fighting season, but Roosevelt's housemen made sure he was around to defend his title. An accusation of stealing apples from the dining hall knocked him down to Grub and guaranteed his availability. Griff's emergence as the baddest brother on campus made him Axel's natural successor. Outside the ring Griff made a hobby of terrorizing the weaker boys, the boys without friends, the weepy ones. Inside the ring his prey stepped right up so he didn't waste time hunting. Like an electric toaster or an automated washing machine, boxing was a modern convenience that made life easier.

The coach for the colored team was a Mississippian named Max David who worked in the school garage. He got an envelope at the end of the year for imparting what he'd learned during his welterweight stint. Max David made his pitch to Griff early in the summer. "My first fight made me cockeyed," he said, "and my farewell fight set my eyes right again, so trust me when I say this sport will break you down to make you better, and that's a fact." Griff smiled. The giant pulverized and unmanned his opponents with cruel inevitability through autumn. He was not graceful, he was not a scientist. He was a powerful instrument of violence, and that sufficed.

Given the typical length of enrollment at Nickel—sabotage by staff aside—most students were only around for one or two fighting seasons. As the championship approached, the Grubs had to be schooled in the importance of those December matches—the prelims inside your dorm, the match between your dorm's guy and the best sluggers from the other two dorms, and then the bout between the best black fighter and whatever chump the white guys put up. The championship would be their sole acquaintance with justice at Nickel.

The combat served as a kind of mollifying spell, to tide them through the daily humiliations. Trevor Nickel instituted the championship matches in 1946, soon after he came on as the director of the Florida Industrial School for Boys with a mandate for reform. Nickel had never run a school before; his background was in agriculture. He made an impression at Klan meetings, however, with his impromptu speeches on moral improvement and the value of work, the disposition of young souls in need of care. The right people remembered his passion when an opening came up. His first Christmas at the school gave the county the chance to witness his improvements. Everything that needed a new coat of paint got a new coat of paint, the dark cells were briefly converted to more innocent use, and the beatings relocated to the small white utility building. Had the good people of Eleanor seen the industrial fan, they might have had a question or two, but the shed was not part of the tour.

Nickel was a longtime boxing evangelist, had steered a lobbying group for its expansion in the Olympics. Boxing had always been popular at the school, as most of the boys had seen their share of scrapes, but the new director took the sport's elevation as his remit. The athletics budget, long an easy target for directors on the skim, was rejiggered to pay for regulation equipment and to bolster the coaching staff. Nickel maintained a general interest in fitness overall. He possessed a fervent belief in the miracle of a human specimen in top shape and often watched the boys shower to monitor the progress of their physical education.

"The director?" Elwood asked when Turner told him that last part.

"Where do you think Dr. Campbell got that trick from?" Turner said. Nickel was gone, but Dr. Campbell, the school psychologist, was known to loiter at the white boys' showers to pick his dates. "All these dirty old men got a club together."

Elwood and Turner were hanging out on the gymnasium bleachers this afternoon. Griff sparred with Cherry, a mulatto who took up boxing as a matter of pedagogy, to teach others how not to speak about his white mother. He was quick and lithe and Griff clobbered him.

Catching Griff at his regimen was Cleveland's favorite occupation those early days in December. Boys from the colored dormitories made the rounds, as well as white scouts from down the hill who wanted the skinny. Griff had been excused from his kitchen shift since Labor Day to train. It was a spectacle. Max kept him on an obscure diet of raw eggs and oats, and stored a jug of what he claimed was goat blood in the icebox. When the coach administered the doses, Griff swallowed the stuff with a lot of theater and mortified the heavy bag in revenge.

Turner had seen Axel fight during his first term at Nickel, two years prior. Axel was slow on his feet but as solid and abiding as an old stone bridge; he weathered what the skies decreed. Contrary to Griff's mealy disposition, he was kind and protective of the smaller kids. "I wonder where he is now," Turner said. "That nigger doesn't have a lick of sense. Making things worse for himself, probably, wherever he is." A Nickel tradition.

Cherry wavered and sank on his ass. Griff spat out his mouthpiece and bellowed. Black Mike stepped into the sparring ring and held Griff's hand up like Lady Liberty's torch.

"Do you think he'll knock him down?" Elwood asked. The likely white contender was a boy named Big Chet, who came from a clan of swamp people and was a bit of a creature.

"Look at those arms, man," Turner said. "Those things are pistons. Or smoked hams."

To see Griff quiver with unspent energy after a match, two chucks unlacing his gloves like retainers, it was hard to imagine how the giant could lose. Which is why, two days later, Turner sat up in surprise when he heard Spencer tell Griff to take a dive.

Turner was napping in the warehouse loft, where he'd

made a nest among crates of industrial scrubbing powder. None of the staff bugged him when he went alone into the big storage room on account of his work with Harper, which meant Turner had a getaway place. No supervisors, no students—just him, a pillow, an army blanket, and Harper's transistor radio. He spent a couple of hours a week up there. It was like when he was tramping and didn't care to know anybody and no one cared to know him. He'd had a few periods like that, when he was rootless and tumbled down the street like an old newspaper. The loft took him back.

The closing of the warehouse door woke him. Then came Griff's dumb donkey voice: "What is it, Mr. Spencer, sir?"

"How's that training coming along, Griff? Good old Max says you're a natural."

Turner frowned. Any time a white man asked you about yourself, they were about to fuck you over. Griff was so stupid he didn't know what was happening. In class, the boy struggled over two plus three, like he didn't know how many damned fingers he had on his hand. Some foolhardies in the schoolhouse laughed at him then and Griff stuck their heads into toilets, one by one over the next week.

Turner's assessment was correct: Griff refused to grasp the reason for the secret meeting. Spencer expounded about the importance of the fight, the tradition of the December match. Then he hinted: Good sportsmanship means letting the other team win sometimes. He tried euphemism: It's like when a tree branch has to bend so it doesn't break. He appealed to fatalism: Sometimes it don't work out, no matter how much you try. But Griff was too thick. *Yes, sir . . . I suppose that's right, Mr. Spencer . . . I believe that is the case, sir.* Finally the superintendent told Griff that his black ass had to take a dive in the third round or else they'd take him out back.

"Yes, sir, Mr. Spencer," Griff said. Up in the loft Turner couldn't see Griff's face, so he didn't know if he understood. The boy had stones in his fists and rocks in his head.

Spencer ended with, "You know you can beat him. That'll have to be enough." He cleared his throat and said, "You come along, now," as if herding a lamb who'd wandered. Turner was alone again.

"Ain't that some shit?" he said. He and Elwood were lounging on Cleveland's front steps after a run to Eleanor. The daylight was thin, winter coming down like the lid on an old pot. Elwood was the only person Turner could tell. The rest of these mutts would blab and then there'd be a lot of busted heads.

Turner had never met a kid like Elwood before. *Sturdy* was the word he returned to, even though the Tallahassee boy looked soft, conducted himself like a goody-goody, and had an irritating tendency to preach. Wore eyeglasses you wanted to grind underfoot like a butterfly. He talked like a white college boy, read books when he didn't have to, and mined them for uranium to power his own personal A-bomb. Still—sturdy.

Elwood wasn't surprised at Turner's news. "Organized boxing is corrupt on every level," he said with authority. "There's been a lot in the newspapers about it." He described what he'd read back at Marconi's, perched on his stool during the dead hours. "Only reason to fix a fight is because you're betting on it."

"I'd bet on it, if I had any money," Turner said. "Sometimes at the Holiday, we put money on the playoffs. I got paid."

"People are going to be upset," Elwood said. Griff's victory was sure to be a feast, but almost as delicious were the morsels the boys traded in anticipation, the scenarios in which the white contender lost control of his bowels or threw up a geyser of blood in Director Hardee's face or white teeth flew from his mouth "like they were chipped out with an ice pick." Fantasies hearty and fortifying.

"Sure," Turner said. "But Spencer says he's going to take you out back, you listen."

"Take him to the White House?"

"I'll show you," Turner said. They had some time before supper.

They walked ten minutes to the laundry, which was shut at this time of day. Turner asked Elwood about the book under his arm and Elwood said a British family was trying to marry off their oldest daughter to keep their estate and title. The story had complicated turns.

"No one wants to marry her? She ugly?"

"She's described as having a handsome face."

"Damn."

Past the laundry were the dilapidated horse stables. The ceiling had given way long ago and nature had crept inside, with skeletal bushes and limp grasses rising in the stalls. You could get up to some wickedness in there if you didn't believe in ghosts, but none of the students had arrived at a definite opinion on the matter so everyone stayed away to be safe. There were two oaks on one side of the stables, with iron rings stabbed into the bark.

"This is *out back*," Turner said. "They say once in a

while they take a black boy here and shackle him up to those. Arms spread out. Then they get a horse whip and tear him up."

Elwood made two fists, then caught himself. "No white boys?"

"The White House, they got that integrated. This place is separate. They take you out back, they don't bring you to the hospital. They put you down as escaped and that's that, boy."

"What about their family?"

"How many boys you know here got family? Or got family that cares about them? Not everyone is you, Elwood." Turner got jealous when Elwood's grandmother visited and brought him snacks, and it slipped out from time to time. Like now. The blinders Elwood wore, walking around. The law was one thing—you can march and wave signs around and change a law if you convinced enough white people. In Tampa, Turner saw the college kids with their nice shirts and ties sit in at the Woolworths. He had to work, but they were out protesting. And it happened—they opened the counter. Turner didn't have the money to eat there either way. You can change the law but you can't change people and how they treat each other. Nickel was racist as hell—half the people who worked here probably dressed up like the Klan on weekends—but the way Turner saw it, wickedness went deeper than skin color. It was Spencer. It was Spencer and it was Griff and it was all the parents who let their children wind up here. It was people.

Which is why Turner brought Elwood out to the two trees. To show him something that wasn't in books.

Elwood grabbed one of the rings and tugged. It was solid,

part of the trunk now. Human bones would break before it came loose.

Harper confirmed the gambling two days later. They'd unloaded a few hogs at Terry's BBQ. "Delivered unto them," Turner said when Harper closed the van door. Their hands reeked of slaughter smell and he asked about the fight.

"I'll put down some money when I see who shakes out for the big one," Harper said. Betting was small-time when Director Nickel ran things—purity of the sport, etc. Nowadays the fat cats turned out, anyone in three counties with a taste for wagering. Well, not anyone, someone on staff had to vouch for you. "You always bet on the colored boy anyway, though. Be foolish not to."

"All boxing is fixed," Elwood said.

"Crooked as a country preacher," Turner added.

"They wouldn't do that," Harper said. This was his childhood he was talking about. He grew up on those matches, chomping popped corn in the VIP section. "It's a beautiful thing."

Turner snorted and started whistling.

The big match was split up over two nights. On the first, the white campus and black campus settled who to send to the main event. For the last two months, three boxing rings had been set up in the gymnasium for training; now only one remained in the center of the big room. It was chilly outside and the spectators stepped into the humid cavern. White men from town claimed the folding chairs closest to the ring, then came staff, and beyond that the student body crammed into the bleachers, squatted on the floors, ashy elbow to ashy elbow. The racial division of the school recreated itself in the gym, with white boys taking the south half and black boys claiming the north. They jostled at the borders.

Director Hardee acted as master of ceremonies. He rarely left his office in the administration building. Turner hadn't seen him since Halloween, when he dressed in a Dracula outfit and distributed sweaty handfuls of candy corn to the younger students. He was a short man, fastened into his suits, with a bald pate that floated in a cloud bank of white hair. Hardee had brought his wife, a robust beauty whose every visit was thoroughly annotated by the students, if furtively—reckless eyeballing called for mandatory beatings. She'd been Miss South Louisiana, or so the story went. She cooled her neck with a paper fan.

The Hardees enjoyed a prime spot in front with the board members. Turner recognized most of them from raking their yards or delivering a ham. Where their pink necks emerged from the linen, that's where you strike, the vulnerable inch.

Harper sat behind the VIP row with the rest of the staff. He carried himself differently in the company of his fellow supervisors, dropping his shirker's affect. Many an afternoon, Turner had seen the man's face and posture click into its proper place when a houseman or supervisor showed up. A snap-to, dropping a disguise or taking one up.

Hardee made a few remarks. The chairman of the board, Mr. Charles Grayson—the manager of the bank and a longtime Nickel supporter—was turning sixty on Friday. Hardee made the students sing "Happy Birthday." Mr. Grayson stood and nodded, hands behind his back like a dictator.

The white dormitories were up first. Big Chet squeezed between the ropes and bounded into the center of the ring.

His cheerleaders expressed themselves with gusto; he commanded a legion. The white boys didn't get it as bad as the black boys, but they were not in Nickel because the world cared overmuch. Big Chet was their Great White Hope. Gossip nailed him for a sleepwalker, punching holes in the bathroom walls without waking. Morning found him sucking on his bloody knuckles. "Nigger looks like Frankenstein," Turner said. Square head, long arms, loping.

The opening fight went three unremarkable rounds. The ref, who managed the floor of the printing plant in the daytime, gave the decision to Big Chet and no one argued otherwise. He was regarded as an even personality, the ref, ever since he slapped a kid and his fraternity ring left the kid half blind. After that he bent a knee to Our Savior and never again raised a hand in anger except at his wife. The white boys' second match opened with a pop—a pneumatic uppercut that whisked Big Chet's opponent into a childhood fear. He spent the remainder of the round and the next two skittering like a rabbit. At the ref's decision, Big Chet rummaged in his mouth and spat out his mouthpiece in two pieces. He raised his big ole arms to the sky.

"I think he could take Griff," Elwood said.

"Maybe he can, but they have to make sure." If you had the power to make people do what you wanted and never exercised it, what was the point of having it?

Griff's bouts with the champs of Roosevelt and Lincoln were brief affairs. Pettibone stood a foot shorter than Griff, an obvious mismatch when you saw them toe to toe, but he'd climbed the Roosevelt heap and that was that. At the bell, Griff barreled out and humiliated his quarry with a battery of *zip-zip-zip* body blows. The crowd winced. "He's having ribs for dinner!" a boy behind Turner shouted. Mrs. Hardee shrieked when Pettibone floated up dreamily on his tippy-toes and then toppled to kiss the dirty mat.

The second match was less lopsided. Griff tenderized the Lincoln boy like a cheap cut of meat for three rounds, but Wilson stayed on his feet to prove his worth to his father. Wilson had two bouts going, the one everybody could see and the one only he could. His father had been dead for years and was thus unable to revise his assessment of his firstborn son's character, but that night Wilson slept without nightmares for the first time in years. The ref gave the fight to Griff with a concerned smile.

Turner surveyed the room and took in the assembled marks, the boys and the bettors. You run a rigged game, you got to give the suckers a taste. Back in Tampa, a few blocks down from the Everetts' house, a street hustler conducted rounds of Find the Lady outside a cigar store. Taking suckers' money all day, weaving those cards around on a cardboard box. The rings on his fingers sparkled and shouted in the sun. Turner liked to hover and take in the show. Track the hustler's eyes, track the mark's eyes as he tried to follow the queen of hearts. Then they turned over their card: How their faces collapsed when they saw they weren't as smart as they thought. The hustler told Turner to beat it, but as the weeks went on he got bored and let the boy hang around. "You got to let them think they know what's going on," he told Turner one day. "They see it with their own eyes, distract themselves with that, so they can't see the bigger game." When the cops hauled him to jail, his cardboard box lay in the alley around the corner for weeks.

With tomorrow's fight set, Turner was transported back

to that street corner. Watching a game of Find the Lady, neither hustler nor mark, outside the game but knowing all its rules. The next evening the white men will put up their money and the black boys will put up their hopes, and then the confidence man turns over the ace of spades and rakes it all in. Turner remembered the excitement of Axel's fight two years ago, the deranged joy in the realization that they were allowed to have something for a change. They were happy for a few hours, spending time in the free world, then it was back to Nickel.

Suckers, all of them.

The morning of Griff's big match, the black students woke up wrung out from sleeplessness and the dining hall bubbled with chatter over the dimension and magnitude of Griff's looming triumph. *That white boy's gonna be toothless as my old granny. The witch doctor can give him the whole bucket of aspirin and he'll still have a headache. The Ku Klux Klan's gonna be crying under their hoods all week.* The colored boys frothed and speculated and stared off in class, slacked off in the sweet potato fields. Mulling the prospect of a black champion: One of them victorious for a change, and those who kept you down whittled to dust, seeing stars.

Griff strutted like a black duke, a gang of chucks in his wake. The younger kids threw punches at their private, invisible adversaries and made up a song about their new hero's prowess. Griff hadn't bloodied or mistreated anyone outside of the ring in a week, as if he'd sworn on a Bible, and Black Mike and Lonnie curbed themselves in solidarity. By all accounts, Griff was unbothered by Spencer's order, or so it seemed to Elwood. "It's like he forgot," he whispered to Turner as they walked to the warehouse after breakfast.

"If I got all this respect, I'd enjoy it, too," Turner said. The next day it would be as if it never happened. He remembered Axel the afternoon after his big fight, stirring a wheelbarrow of cement, gloomy and diminished once more. "When's the next time fools who hate and fear you are going to treat you like Harry Belafonte?"

"Or he forgot," Elwood said.

That evening they filed into the gymnasium. Some of the kitchen boys operated a big kettle, cranking out popcorn and scooping it into paper cones. The chucks chomped it down and raced to the back of the line for seconds. Turner, Elwood, and Jaimie squeezed together in the middle of the bleachers. It was a good spot. "Hey Jaimie, aren't you supposed to be sitting over there?" Turner asked.

Jaimie grinned. "Way I see it, I win either way."

Turner crossed his arms and scanned the faces on the floor. There was Spencer. He shook hands with the fat cats in the front row, the director and his wife, and then sat with the staff, smug and sure. He withdrew a silver flask from his windbreaker and took a pull. The bank manager handed out cigars. Mrs. Hardee took one and everyone watched her blow smoke. Wispy gray figures twirled in the overhead light, living ghosts.

On the other side of the room, the white boys stomped their feet on the wood and the thunder bounced off the walls. The black boys picked it up and the stomping rolled around the room in a staggered stampede. It traveled a full circuit before the boys stopped and cheered at their racket.

"Send him to the undertaker!"

The ref rang the bell. The two fighters were the same height and build, hacked from the same quarry. An even match, the track record of colored champions notwithstanding. Those opening rounds, there was no dancing or ducking. The boys bit into each other again and again, trading attacks, bucking the pain. The crowd bellowed and jeered at every advance and reversal. Black Mike and Lonnie hung on the ropes, hooting scatological invective at Big Chet, until the ref kicked their hands away. If Griff feared knocking out Big Chet by accident, he gave no sign. The black giant battered the white boy without mercy, absorbed his opponent's counterassault, jabbed at the kid's face as if punching his way through the wall of a prison cell. When blood and sweat blinded him, he maintained an eerie sense of Big Chet's position and fended the boy off.

At the end of the second round, you had to call the fight for Griff, despite Big Chet's admirable offensives.

"Making it look good," Turner said.

Elwood frowned in disdain at the whole performance, which made Turner smile. The fight was as rigged and rotten as the dishwashing races he'd told Turner about, another gear in the machine that kept black folks down. Turner enjoyed his friend's new bend toward cynicism, even as he found himself swayed by the magic of the big fight. Seeing Griff, their enemy and champion, put a hurting on that white boy made a fellow feel all right. In spite of himself. Now that the third and final round was upon them, he wanted to hold on to that feeling. It was real—in their blood and minds—even if it was a lie. Turner was certain Griff was going to win even though he knew he wasn't. Turner was a mark after all, another sucker, but he didn't care.

Big Chet advanced on Griff and unfurled a series of quick jabs that drove him into his corner. Griff was trapped and Turner thought, *Now*. But the black boy gathered his opponent in a clinch and remained on his feet. Body blows sent the white boy reeling. The round dwindled into seconds and Griff did not relent. Big Chet squashed his nose with a thunk and Griff shook it off. Each time Turner saw the perfect moment to take a dive—Big Chet's rigorous assault would cover even the worst acting—Griff refused the opening.

Turner nudged Elwood, who had a look of horror on his face. They saw it: Griff wasn't going down. He was going to go for it.

No matter what happened after.

When the bell sounded for the last time, the two Nickel boys in the ring were entwined, bloody and slick, propping each other up like a human tepee. The ref split them and they stumbled crazily to their corners, spent.

Turner said, "Damn."

"Maybe they called it off," Elwood said.

Sure, it was possible the ref was in on it and they'd decided to fix it that way instead. Spencer's reaction dispelled that theory. The superintendent was the only person in the second row still sitting, a malignant scowl screwed into his face. One of the fat cats turned around, red-faced, and grabbed his arm.

Griff jerked to his feet, lumbered to the center of the ring, and shouted. The noise of the crowd smothered his words. Black Mike and Lonnie held back their friend, who appeared to have lost his wits. He struggled to cross the ring.

The ref called for everyone to settle down and delivered his decision: The first two rounds went to Griff, the last to Big Chet. The black boys had prevailed.

Instead of cavorting around the canvas in triumph, Griff

squirmed free and traversed the ring to where Spencer sat. Now Turner heard his words: "I thought it was the second! I thought it was the second!" He was still screaming as the black boys led him back to Roosevelt, cheering and whooping for their champion. They had never seen Griff cry before and took his tears for those of triumph.

Getting hit in the head can rattle your brains. Getting hit in the head like that can make you addle-minded and confused. Turner never thought it'd make you forget two plus one. But Griff had never been good at arithmetic, he supposed.

He was all of them in one black body that night in the ring, and all of them when the white men took him out back to those two iron rings. They came for Griff that night and he never returned. The story spread that he was too proud to take a dive. That he refused to kneel. And if it made the boys feel better to believe that Griff escaped, broke away and ran off into the free world, no one told them otherwise, although some noted that it was odd the school never sounded the alarm or sent out the dogs. When the state of Florida dug him up fifty years later, the forensic examiner noted the fractures in the wrists and speculated that he'd been restrained before he died, in addition to the other violence attested by the broken bones.

Most of those who know the story of the rings in the trees are dead by now. The iron is still there. Rusty. Deep in the heartwood. Testifying to anyone who cares to listen.

CHAPTER TEN

Miscreants had bashed in the reindeers' heads. They expected a certain amount of wear and tear after the holiday, when the boys gathered to pack the delicate Christmas displays. Bent antlers, a leg twisting from shreds at the joint. What lay before them was malicious vandalism.

"Look at this," Miss Baker said. She sucked her teeth. Miss Baker was on the young side for a Nickel teacher, with a predilection for simmering outrage. At Nickel, her dependable ire stemmed from the regrettable condition of the colored art room, the haphazard supplies, and what could only be interpreted as institutional resistance to her various improvements. The young teachers never lasted long before they moved on. "All this hard work."

Turner pulled out the balled-up newspaper from the reindeer skull and unwrinkled it. The headline rendered a verdict on the first Nixon and Kennedy debate: ROUT. "This one's a goner," he said.

Elwood raised his hand. "Do you want us to make all new ones or just new heads, Miss Baker?"

"I think the bodies we can salvage," she said. She grimaced and twisted her curly red hair into a bun. "Just do the heads. Touch up the fur on the bodies and next year we'll start from scratch."

Visitors from all over the panhandle, families from Georgia and Alabama caravaned every year to take in the annual Christmas Fair. It was the pride of the administration, a fund-raising bounty that proved reform was no mere lofty notion but a workable proposition. A bit of an operation, gears and gears. Five miles of colored lights dangled from the cedars and traced the roofs of the south campus. The thirty-foot Santa at the foot of the drive required a crane to fit it together. The assembly instructions for the miniature steam train that looped around the football field were passed through the decades like the scrolls of a solemn sect.

Last year's display attracted more than a hundred thousand guests to the property. There was no reason, Director Hardee insisted, that the good boys of the Nickel Academy couldn't improve on that number.

The white students handled construction and the reassembly of the large displays—the gigantic sleigh, the Nativity diorama, the train tracks—and the black students did most of the painting. Touch-ups, new additions. Correcting the artistic errors of previous, less meticulous boys and refurbing the old workhorses. Three-foot-high candy canes lined each dormitory walkway, and they invariably required new dabs of red and white paint. The monstrous poster-size Christmas cards featured North Pole shenanigans, fairytale favorites like Hansel and Gretel and the Three Little Pigs, and biblical re-creations. The cards tilted on stands along the school roads as if adorning the lobby of a grand theater.

The students loved this time of year, whether it reminded them of Christmases back home, miserable as they were, or it was the first real holiday of their whole lives. Everyone got gifts—Jackson County was generous that way—white and black alike, not just sweaters and underwear but baseball gloves and boxes of tin army men. For one morning they were like boys from nice houses in nice neighborhoods where it was quiet at night and nightmareless.

Even Turner had cause to smile, as he touched up the Gingerbread Man card and remembered the folk hero's rallying cry: "You can't catch me, you can't catch me." A good way to be. He didn't remember how the story ended.

Miss Baker signed off on his work and he joined Jaimie, Elwood, and Desmond over by the papier-mâché station.

Desmond whispered, "Jaimie says Earl."

Desmond found the stuff but Jaimie came up with the scheme. It was an unlikely proposition from a student who had just made it to Pioneer. Almost out. Jaimie grew up in Tallahassee like Elwood, but they couldn't name two places they had in common. Different neighborhoods, different cities. His father, he'd been told, was a full-time flimflam man and the part-time regional salesman for a vacuum cleaner company, driving his circuit around the panhandle and knocking on doors. It wasn't clear how he met Jaimie's mother, but Jaimie was one proof of their acquaintance and the vacuum cleaner that they lugged from short-term residence to short-term residence was another.

Jaimie's mother, Ellie, swept up at the Coca-Cola bottling plant on South Monroe, in All Saints. Jaimie and his gang used to kick around the railroad yard nearby. Playing craps, passing around a harrowed copy of *Playboy*. He was a good kid, not the most diligent about school attendance, but never would've seen the inside of Nickel if not for the depot. An old rummy who haunted the yards stuck his hand down the pants of one of the gang and they beat him senseless. Jaimie was the only one who didn't outrun the deputies.

During his term at Nickel, the Mexican boy sidestepped the squabbles that embroiled the rest of them, the uncounted disputes over psychological turf and endless encroachments. His constant dorm reassignments notwithstanding, Jaimie kept a quiet profile and conducted himself in accordance with the Nickel handbook's rules of conduct—a miracle, since no one had ever seen the handbook despite its constant invocations by the staff. Like justice, it existed in theory.

Spiking a supervisor's drink lay outside his personality.

Nonetheless: Earl.

Desmond worked in the sweet potato fields. No complaints. He liked the way the potatoes smelled at the cusp of picking time, that warm, peaty scent. Like his father's sweat when he came home from work and made sure Desmond was tucked in proper.

The previous week Desmond was part of a team ordered to rearrange a work shed, the big gray one where they kept the tractors. Half the lights were burned out and critters had made a home in various spots. Spiderwebs canopied one corner and Desmond stabbed a broom at the white blossoms, wary of what might burst forth. He recognized some of the loose cans stacked there and found a place for them, but there was one green relic too faded to read. He shook it: solid throughout. He asked one of the older boys what to do with it, and the kid said that it shouldn't be in there. "That's horse medicine, to make them puke when they eat something they shouldn't." The old stables were nearby—perhaps that junk had ended up here when they closed them down. At Nickel, things tended to end up where they were supposed to, but a lazy or mischievous soul occasionally subverted the order.

Desmond hid the medicine in his windbreaker and took it to Cleveland.

One of them—no one remembered who, when it was all over—suggested putting it in a staffer's drink. Why else had Desmond taken it? But it was Jaimie who made the scheme real in his calm rebuttals to the counterarguments. "Who would you give it to?" Jaimie asked his friends in turn, with a rhetorical air. Jaimie had a stutter that slunk out when he asked questions—he had an uncle with a quick hand—but the stutter disappeared during the can discussions.

Desmond fingered Patrick, a houseman who'd beat him for wetting his bed and made him drag his soiled mattress to the laundry in the middle of the night. "That fucking peckerwood—I'd like to see him puke up his guts."

They were in the Cleveland rec room, after school let out. No one else around. Occasionally cheers from one of the sports fields wafted over. *Who would you give it to?* Elwood suggested Duggin. No one knew that he and Duggin had had a dustup. Duggin was a stout-backed white man who stomped around with a sleepy, cow-eyed look. He had a way of suddenly appearing in front of you, like a puddle or a pothole, and you learned that his big meaty hands were faster than you'd think, pincering shoulder blades, noosing a skinny neck. The supervisor, Elwood told them, had socked him in the stomach for talking to a white student, a kid he'd met in the hospital. Fraternization between the students of the two campuses was discouraged. The boys nodded—"makes sense"—but they all knew he really wanted to give it to Spencer. For his legs. No one dared mention Spencer's name anywhere near this daydream or else they'd never have wasted a breath on it.

"I'd give it to Wainwright," Turner said. He told them how Wainwright had caught him smoking cigarettes, back during his first term at Nickel. Knocked him upside the head so hard it left a lump on his cheek. Wainwright was pale-skinned, but all the black boys knew from his hair and nose that he had some Negro blood. He beat the black boys for knowing what he pretended not to know about himself. "I was greener than you, El, back then." No one had caught him smoking since.

It was Jaimie's turn. He said simply, "Earl," and did not elaborate.

Why?

"He knows."

The days passed and they picked up the prank between checkers and Ping-Pong. Different targets emerged when they saw another student mistreated or suddenly remembered some personal encounter, a reprimand, a box on the ear. One name remained constant: Earl. Elwood dropped Duggin from his rotation and threw in Earl one day. Earl hadn't beat Elwood the night they took him to the White House, but he was not-Spencer, Spencer once removed. Close enough.

It's possible Elwood already knew the answer when he asked, "What's the Holiday Luncheon?"

The Holiday Luncheon was marked on the big calendar in the dorm's entrance hall. Desmond said it wasn't for them, it was for the staff. A nice meal in the dining hall to celebrate another year of hard work on the north campus.

"And they get to raid the meat lockers for some prime

beef to give themselves," Turner said. Boys volunteered for the opportunity to rack up merits by serving as waiters.

Desmond said, "That would be a good time to do it." Saying it and not saying it.

Jaime, as ever, said, "Earl."

Earl sometimes worked the south campus, sometimes the north. Under most circumstances, they'd have heard about the bad blood between Jaimie and the supervisor but both of them spent time on the white half and who knew what had passed between them down there. It could have been Lovers' Lane, some back talk, a frame-up by one of the white boys. Earl was a regular at the drinking sessions at the motor pool. When the motor-pool light was on at night and you heard them carrying on, you prayed you didn't have a beating hanging over your head or that you'd been picked for a date on Lovers' Lane. It would end up bad.

Strange medicine in an old green can. The boys gathered the words and intonations of a justice spell. Justice or revenge. No one wanted to admit it was a real plan they cooked up all along. They kept returning to it as Christmas approached, passing the idea between them so each considered its heft and cast. As the prank evolved from abstraction to something more solid, full of hows and whens and what-ifs, Desmond, Turner, and Jaimie stopped including Elwood without realizing it. The prank was against his moral conscience. Hard to picture the Reverend Martin Luther King Jr. dosing Governor Orval Faubus with a couple of ounces of lye. And Elwood's beating at the White House had him scarred all over, not just his legs. It had weeviled deep into his personality. The way his shoulders sank when Spencer appeared, the flinch and shrink. He could only stand so much talk of revenge before the reality grabbed ahold of him.

Then it popped and the boys talked about it no more. "They'd put us in the ground," Desmond said, when Jaimie sparked up another round of "who do we get."

"We have to be careful," Jaimie said.

"I'm going to play some basketball," Desmond said, and he was out.

Turner sighed. He had to admit that the game had gotten boring. It was nice for a time to picture one of their tormentors puking all over their yummy spread at the Holiday Luncheon, spraying all those peckerwoods with his mess. Shitting his pants, face gone strawberry-red from pain, heaving until what came out wasn't food but his own dark blood. A pleasant vision, a different kind of medicine. But they weren't going to do it, and that fact spoiled it. Turner stood, and Jaimie shook his head and joined them for basketball.

Friday, the day of the Holiday Luncheon, the Community Service crew was out on rounds. Harper, Turner, and Elwood had just finished up with the five-and-ten when the supervisor said he had something he had to do. "I'll be back in a hot minute," he told them. "Y'all can wait here."

The van disappeared. Turner and Elwood walked up the scrabbly alley to the street. Harper had left them alone before, when they were working on a board member's house. Never on Main Street. Even after two months of back-alley exchanges, Elwood was incredulous. "We can walk around?" he asked Turner.

"We don't got to make a commotion, but yeah," Turner said, pretending it had happened before plenty of times.

Sightings of Nickel students on Main Street were not uncommon. The students shuffled off the gray school buses in their state-issued denim for community service—real community service, not the special services of Turner and Elwood's assignments—cleaning up rubbish in the park after July Fourth fireworks or the Founders Day parade. Once a season the choir visited the Baptist church to show off their beautiful voices as Director Hardee's secretaries handed out envelopes for donations. A boy might be found in the company of a supervisor darting into town for business. Two unescorted colored boys was a sight, however. It was lunch hour. The white people of Eleanor tried to account for them. The boys didn't look shifty or scared. Their supervisor was probably inside the hardware store—Mr. Bontemps hated niggers and had made them wait outside. The white folks walked on. It wasn't their business.

Christmas toys—windup robots and air guns and painted trains—filled the front window of the five-and-ten. The boys knew to hide their enthusiasm over little-kid things that still had an allure. They walked quickly past the bank. It seemed like a place where board members might appear, or at least white men with power who signed official documents, like reform school orders.

"It's weird being out here," Elwood said.

"It's okay," Turner said.

"No one watching," Elwood said.

The sidewalk was empty, a break in the noon traffic. Turner looked around and smiled. He knew what Elwood was thinking. "Most of them talk about running into the swamp," Turner said. "Wash their scent off so the dogs can't get them, then hide in there until the coast is clear and hitch somewhere. West or north. That's how they get you, though, because that's where everybody runs to. And you can't wash no scent off, that's only in movies."

"How would you do it?"

Turner had turned it over in his head many times but had never shared it with anyone. "You head out here into the free world, not the swamp. Snatch clothes from a clothesline. Head south, not north, because they ain't expecting it. Those empty houses we pass on our deliveries? Mr. Tolliver's house—he's always down at the capital for business. His house is empty. You raid them for supplies and then put as many miles between you and the dogs as you can, tire them out. The trick is not doing what they know you going to do." Then he remembered the most important part. "And don't take no one with you. Not one of those dummies. They'll take you down with them."

They had ambled to the front of the pharmacy. Behind the window, a blond woman crouched over a carriage and spooned ice cream into her baby's mouth. The little boy was a mess, smeared with chocolate and bawling with happiness.

"You got any money?" Turner said.

"More than you got," Elwood said.

No money at all. They laughed because they knew the drugstore didn't serve colored patrons, and sometimes laughter knocked out a few bricks from the barricade of segregation, so tall and so wide. And they laughed because ice cream was the last thing they wanted.

Elwood's aversion was understandable; the visit to the Ice Cream Factory had left its marks. Turner hated the stuff on account of his aunt's boyfriend, who moved in with them when Turner was eleven years old. Mavis was his mother's sister and his only family. The state of Florida didn't know about her, thus the blank space on their forms where her name should have been written, but he had lived with her for a time. His father, Clarence, was a bit of a "rambler," not that he had to be told because he had the same affliction. Turner remembered him as two big brown hands and a raspy chuckle. When he heard autumn leaves scuttling in the wind, he remembered that chuckle. The same way Nickel boys remembered White House visits when they heard the smart snap of leather, decades later.

Turner last saw his father when he was three years old. After that, the man was the wind. His mother, Dorothy, hung around longer, long enough for her to choke on her own vomit. She had that taste—rotgut, the rougher the better. The stuff she drank the night she died left her twisted and blue and cold on the front-room sofa. He knew where she was now—six feet under in St. Sebastian Cemetery—which was one thing he had on his upstanding friend Elwood. Elwood's mother and father had lit out West and didn't even send a postcard. What kind of mother leaves her kid in the middle of the night? One that doesn't give a shit. He made a note to save that as a low blow if he and Elwood ever got into a real fight. Turner knew his mother loved him. She just loved liquor more.

His aunt Mavis took him in and made sure Turner had nice clothes for school and three meals. The last Saturday of every month she wore her good red dress and sprayed perfume into her neck and went out with her girlfriends, but apart from that her life was the hospital, where she worked as a nurse, and Turner. No one had ever called her pretty. She had tiny black eyes, an afterthought for a chin, and when Ishmael started courting her, she fell quick. He called her pretty and a lot of other things she'd never heard before. Ishmael was a maintenance man at the Houston airport and when he came by with flowers they almost hid the industrial odor that permeated his skin no matter how much he washed.

Ishmael was a man of secret menace who stored up violence like a battery; Turner learned to recognize these men from then on. How Mavis brightened at the thought of him, singing ditties from the movie musicals she loved, locking herself in the hall bathroom with a hot comb while the transistor crackled. In and out of tune. It never occurred to Turner why she wore sunglasses two weeks straight that one time, why she stayed in her room some mornings and didn't emerge until past noon, limping with soft moans.

The day after Turner put himself between Mavis and Ishmael's fists, Ishmael took him out for ice cream. A. J. Smith's, over on Market Street. "Bring this young man the biggest sundae you got." Every bite like a sock in the mouth. He ate every miserable spoonful and ever since it struck him that adults are always trying to buy off children to make them forget their bad actions. Had the flavor of that fact in his mouth when he ran from his aunt's house that last time.

Nickel served the students vanilla ice cream once a month, and it made them so squealingly happy, like a bunch of dumb piglets in a sty, that Turner wanted to knock everyone flat. Third Wednesday of the month, Turner and Elwood carried most of the north campus's ice-cream allotment through the back door of the Eleanor pharmacy. Turner felt he was performing a service for his fellow students, sparing them.

The blond lady pushed the carriage toward the door and Elwood held the door open for her. She didn't say a word.

Harper pulled up and waved them to the front seat. "You boys up to no good?"

"Yes, sir," Turner said. He whispered to Elwood, "Don't go stealing my plan, now, El. That shit's pure gold." They got in the van.

When they drove past the administration building toward the colored campus, the students stood in worried huddles on the green. Harper slowed and called over one of the white boys. "What's happening?"

"They took Mr. Earl to the hospital. Something's wrong with him."

Harper parked the van by the warehouse and ran to the hospital. Elwood and Turner hustled to Cleveland. Elwood scanning every which way like a squirrel and Turner trying to maintain a front, which made him move like a space robot. They needed a report. Despite the segregated campuses, the black boys and white boys passed on news for safety's sake. Sometimes Nickel was like being back home, where the older brother or sister that you hated warned you about a parent's black mood or daylong drinking jag so you could make preparations.

They found Desmond outside the colored dining hall. Turner looked inside. The staff table was still set in the aftermath. Half set—the overturned chairs pointed to a fuss, and the smear of blood showed where they'd dragged out Earl.

"I don't think it was medicine," Desmond said. His deep voice added a baleful tone.

Turner punched him in the shoulder. "You're going to get us killed!"

"It wasn't me! It wasn't me!" Desmond said. He looked over Turner's shoulder toward the White House.

Elwood's hand covered his mouth. There was a half of a work-shoe footprint in the blood. He snapped to and turned downhill. To see if they were coming for them. "Where's Jaimie?"

"That nigger," Desmond said.

They strategized on the dining-hall steps. Turner suggested that they hang out and gather information on Earl's condition from the other students. He didn't say he wanted to stay there because it was a straight shot to the road bordering the east side of campus. If Spencer came up with a posse, he'd be out lickety-split. *Can't catch me, I'm the Gingerbread Man.*

Jaimie showed up an hour later, looking rumpled and a bit dazed, like he'd just had a turn on a Tilt-A-Whirl. He completed the story they'd got from the other boys. The Holiday Luncheon commenced as it always did. The special tablecloth that only got aired out once a year covered the staff table, the nice dishes were wiped of dust. The supervisors took their places and drank beer, sharing rowdy stories and off-color speculation about the bustier secretaries and teachers. It was loud and they enjoyed themselves. A few minutes into the meal, Earl bolted up and grabbed his stomach. They thought he was choking. Then he commenced to disperse his insides in a spray. When the blood appeared they carried him down the hill to the hospital.

Jaimie told them that he waited among the boys outside the ward until the ambulance took him away.

"You're crazy," Elwood said.

"I didn't do it," Jaimie said. His face was blank. "I was playing football. Everybody saw me."

"The can is gone from my locker," Desmond said.

"I told you I didn't take it," Jaimie said. "Maybe someone robbed your shit and they did it." He knocked Desmond's shoulder. "You said it was horse medicine!"

"That's what he told me," Desmond said. "You saw it—it had a horse on it."

"Could have been a goat," Turner said.

"Maybe it was horse poison," Elwood said.

"Or goat poison," Turner added.

"They ain't rats, dummy," Desmond said. "You shoot horses, not poison them."

"He's lucky he ain't dead then," Jaimie said. Elwood and Desmond continued to press him, but his version did not change.

It was hard to miss the smile that tugged at Jaimie's mouth from time to time. Turner wasn't angry that Jaimie lied to their faces. He admired liars who kept on lying even though their lies were obvious, but there was nothing anyone could do about it. Another proof of one's powerlessness before other people. Jaimie wasn't going to admit it, so Turner just watched the boys and the activity down the hill.

Earl didn't die. He didn't come back to work, either. Doctor's orders. They'd hear about that in the coming days. And a few weeks after that, they'd discover that Earl's replacement, a tall man named Hennepin, was made of meaner stuff, and he'd subject many a boy to his cruel whims. But they made it through that first evening without being strung up, and when word came that Dr. Cooke blamed

Earl's fit on his constitution—he had a family history, it seemed—Turner stopped strategizing his escape.

Just before lights-out, he and Elwood were hanging out by the big oak in front of the dormitory. The campus had quieted. Turner wanted a cigarette, but his pack was back in the warehouse loft. He whistled instead, that Elvis song Harper kept singing on their runs.

The night bugs started up in a wave. "Earl," Turner said. "That's some shit."

"Wish I'd been there to see it, though," Elwood said.

"Ha."

"I wish it had been Spencer," Elwood said. "That would have been nice." His palm went to the back of his thigh, to the spot he rubbed when he remembered.

They heard a whoop. Down the hill, the supervisors had turned on the Christmas lights and the boys got a look at the results of all the hard work of the last few weeks. Green, red, and white bulbs sketched a route of holiday cheer along the trees and the south-campus buildings. Far off in the dark, the big Santa at the entrance glowed from the inside with a demonic fire.

"Those are some lights," Turner said.

Past the White House, blinking lights outlined the old water tower—one of the white kids had fallen from the ladder while nailing them up and had broken his collarbone. The lights floated on the *X*'s of the wooden struts, circled the huge tank, sketched the triangular peak. Like a spaceship taking off. It reminded Turner of something, then it came to him—that amusement park, Fun Town, from the TV commercials. That dumb, happy music, the bumper cars and the roller coaster, and the Atomic Rocket. The other boys talked about the place from time to time, they'd go there when they were out in the free world again. Turner thought that was stupid. They didn't let colored people in those nice places. But there it was before him, pointed at the stars, decked in a hundred flickering lights, waiting for takeoff: a rocket. Launched in darkness toward another dark planet they couldn't see.

"It looks nice," Turner said.

"We did a good job," Elwood said.

PART Three

CHAPTER ELEVEN

"Elwood?"

He grunted in response from the living room, where the window kept a sliver of Broadway below: Sammy's Shoe Repair, the closed-down travel agency, and the median that ran up the avenue. The angle of his vision made a trapezoid, his personal snow globe of the city. It was a good place to smoke and he'd found a way to perch on the sill that didn't aggravate his back.

"I'm going out for a bag of ice, I can't take it anymore," Denise said, and locked the front door behind her. He had given her a set of keys last week.

He didn't mind the heat. This city knew how to concoct a miserable summer, sure, but it had nothing on the South on those hot days. The way New Yorkers complained about summer heat, on the subway, in the bodega, made him snicker ever since he got here. There was a garbage strike then, too, his first day in the city, but it had been February. It didn't smell as bad. This time whenever he left the vestibule downstairs, the stench was a thicket—he wanted a machete to hack through it. It was only the second day of the strike.

The wildcat strike of '68: an introduction to the city so

wretched that he had to interpret it as a hazing. Steel trash cans mobbed the pavement—overflowing and untouched for days—and the newer garbage in bundled bags and cardboard boxes huddled against them. He avoided public transportation in a new place until he got the lay of it and he'd never been on a subway before. He walked all the way uptown from the Port Authority. Walking in a straight line was impossible. He weaved around the mounds of refuse. When he got to the Statler, the SRO on Ninety-Ninth Street, the residents had kicked open a path to the front door between two monstrous piles of garbage. Rats zipped back and forth. If you wanted to break into one of the second-floor rooms, all you had to do was scale the trash.

The manager gave him a key to a place in the back, four flights up. Hot plate, with a bathroom down the hall. One of the guys he worked with in Baltimore told him about the flophouse and painted a terrible picture. It wasn't as bad as the guy made it out. He'd stayed in worse places. After a couple of days, he bought cleanser at the A&P and took it on himself to clean the toilet and shower. No one else bothered—that kind of joint. He'd scrubbed dirty johns plenty of times, plenty of places.

On his knees in the stink. Welcome to New York.

Down on Broadway, Denise crossed his perch view. Seen from street level, the median was clean most days. From the third floor you peered over the benches and trees and saw the trash crowding the subway ventilation grates and paving stones. Paper bags and beer bottles and tabloids. Now the crap was everywhere, in drifts. With the latest strike under way, everybody saw what he saw all the time: The city was a mess.

He stubbed out his smoke in the teacup and made it to the couch without hitting one of those gongs. Ever since he put his back out, he'd feel all right and forget and move too fast and then *gong*—a detonation in his spine. *Gong* while sitting on the toilet, *gong* while picking up his pants. He yelped like a dog and then curled on the floor for a few minutes. The bathroom tile cool on his skin. It was his own fault. You never knew what was in those drawers and boxes. One time when they were moving this old Ukrainian guy—a cop who got his pension and picked up stakes to Philadelphia where he had a niece—he bent down to lift a night table and his spine popped. Larry said he heard it from the hallway. The cop kept his free weights in there. Three hundred pounds of weights, in case he got the urge to lift in the middle of the night. What put his back out last week was a big wooden bureau, harmless-looking, but he'd been working extra shifts for money. Sleepy and sloppy. "You got to watch it with that Danish modern shit," Larry told him. When Denise returned he'd ask her to fill another hot-water bottle, long as she was going to be in the kitchen fixing more rum and Cokes.

The block was loud most nights with salsa music and it was louder this evening, what with everyone keeping their windows open because of the heat, plus tomorrow was July Fourth. Everyone had off. If his back wasn't too troublesome, they were going to Coney Island for the fireworks, but tonight they would stay in and watch *The Defiant Ones* on channel 4. Sidney Poitier and Tony Curtis, two convicts chained together on the run through the swamp, dodging hunting dogs and dumb-faced deputies with shotguns. Phony Hollywood crap, but he always watched the movie when it came on, usually on *The Late Late Show*, and Denise liked Sidney Poitier.

His rooms were furnished with castoffs from work. A kind of showroom for the furniture of New Yorkers from all over the city, in rotation, new stuff coming in and old stuff going out. His queen-size bed with the type of super-stiff mattress he liked, the dresser with the fancy brass studs, all the lamps and rugs. People get rid of plenty when they move—sometimes they're changing not just places but personalities. Up or down "the economic ladder." Maybe the bed won't fit in the new place, or the sofa's too boxy, or they're newlyweds and put a new living-room set on their registry. A lot of these white-flight families splitting for the suburbs, Long Island and Westchester, they're making a whole new start—shaking the city off, and that means getting rid of how they used to see themselves. Him and the rest of the crew from Horizon Moving had dibs before the junkman got his hands on it. The couch he lay on now was his twelfth in seven years. Constantly upgrading. One of the perks of working for a moving company, though it was hell on your back sometimes.

Even if he scavenged furniture like a transient, he put down roots. After his childhood home, this was the place he'd lived the longest. He started this New York stint at the SRO, stayed there a few months until he got the job at 4 Brothers washing dishes. He moved around a bunch—uptown, Spanish Harlem—until he got a line on the job at Horizon, steady work, and humped it down here to Eighty-Second Street off Broadway. He knew he was going to take the apartment when the landlord threw the door wide: here. Four years and counting. "I'm middle class now," he joked to himself. Even the roaches were of a noble sort, scurrying when he turned on the bathroom light instead of ignoring his presence. He took their modesty as a touch of class.

Denise returned. "Did you hear me outside?" She went into the kitchen and stabbed the bag of ice with a butter knife.

"What?"

"This rat ran across my feet and I screamed. That was me," she said.

Denise was tall and Harlem-tough and could've played basketball in one of the lady leagues. One of these city girls who wasn't afraid of anything. He'd seen her curse out this muscle-bound turkey who whispered something untoward as she passed on the street, she got up in the dude's face, but a rat made her squeal like a little girl. Denise was most definitely not a little girl, so when she let out that part of her it was always a surprise. She lived on 126th next to a vacant lot and the heat and now the garbage made the empty lot livelier than usual. The bastards were everywhere, bursting out of their underground hidey-holes. She said she saw a rat as big as a dog last night. "Barked like one, too." He opined that maybe it was a dog, but she wasn't going back today and he was glad to have her.

Her Wednesday-night classes were canceled because of the Fourth. He was off, too, that afternoon, sleeping when she came over and got into bed with him. Her big silver earrings on the bedside table—courtesy of the Atkinson family, Turtle Bay to York Avenue, three kids and a dog and a Gimbels dining-room set—woke him up. By now she knew the spot on his back where it hurt and kneaded it and then told him to roll over and got on top. The room was ten degrees hotter when they were done and well tangled up in each other. Warm rum and Cokes worked for a while and then they didn't and an ice run was in order.

They met at the high school up on 131st Street. At night there were adult classes. He was working on his GED and she taught ESL to Dominicans and Poles in the classroom next door. He waited to finish the course before he asked her out. Earned his certificate and feeling proud and it was one of those moments that makes you realize you have no one in your life who cares about the occasional triumph. He'd had the thought of getting his GED in the back of his mind for a while. Tended to it like it was a candle flame cupped in his hand out of the wind. He kept seeing the ads on the subway—Complete Your Studies at Night on Your Own Terms—and was so happy to get that piece of paper that he said, Fuck it, and walked right up to her. Big brown eyes and a bridge of freckles over her nose. *On His Own Terms.* He hardly ever did it any other way.

Asked her out and she said no. She was seeing someone. Then a month later she called him up and they went out for Cuban Chinese.

Denise brought over the rum and Cokes with ice. "And I got us some sandwiches," she said.

He set up the TV tray, which had been left behind by Mr. Waters when he picked up stakes from Amsterdam Avenue to Arthur Avenue in the Bronx. It folded up so that it fit neat between the couch and the end table, like that. Nobel Prize in Physics to the guy who invented it.

"They need to get off their asses and pick it all up," Denise said from the kitchen. "Beame has to pick up the phone and talk to these people."

She thought the mayor was a bum and relished the strike

for its opportunity of complaint. She listed her gripes as he wrangled the rabbit ears to the best place for channel 4. The smell, she said, for one—of the rotting food and the bleach the supers sprayed on top of it. The bleach was for the flies that swarmed over the piles of trash in a gross haze and for the maggots twisting on the pavement. Then there was the smoke. People lit the garbage on fire to get rid of it—he didn't understand this, and he considered himself a student of the human animal—and the limp breezes between the buildings carried the smoke all over. The fire engines screamed as they scattered across the city on the avenues and side streets.

That, plus the rats.

He sighed. In every argument he took whatever side stuck it to the Man, rule one. Cops and politicians, fat-cat businessmen and judges, the assorted motherfuckers working levers. "They got 'em by the balls, they should twist," he said. "They're working men." Mayor Beame, Nixon and his bullshit, it was almost enough to make him want to vote. But he avoided the government whenever possible so as not to push his little bit of luck.

"Why don't you sit down, baby," he said. "I'll get it together."

"I already did it all." Even put the kettle on for his hot-water bottle. It whistled.

Trash-fire smoke snuck in through the window so he opened the one in the bedroom for cross ventilation. She was right. It'd be a true hassle if this strike went as long as the last one. It was terrible out there. But it was good for the rest of the city to see what kind of place they were really living in.

Try his perspective for a change. See how they liked it.

The news anchor offered the holiday weather and gave a brief update on the strike—"talks continue"—and told the viewers to stay tuned for the *Nine O'Clock Movie.*

He tapped her glass with his. "You're married to me, now—here's the ring."

"What?"

"From the movie. Sidney Poitier says it." Holding up the chains that bind him to the redneck.

"You should watch what you say."

Sure, the dialogue changed depending on who was saying it and who you said it to. Like the ending of the movie. On the one hand, neither convict made it out. Or you look at it the other way and each of them could've made it to freedom if they'd let the other one die. Maybe it didn't matter—they were fucked either way. He stopped watching the movie a few years later when he realized he didn't watch it because it was sort of corny, or they got the facts wrong, or it marked how far he had come, but because watching it made him sad, and a nutjob part of him sought out that sadness. At a certain point he learned the smarter play was to avoid the things that brought you low.

That night, though, he didn't see the end of the movie because Denise wore a denim skirt and her big thighs sticking out distracted him too much. He reached over when that antacid commercial came on.

The Defiant Ones, then sex, then sleep. Fire engines in the night. Tomorrow morning he had to get up and out, back pain or no, because at ten he was going to meet the man and buy the van. He had a roll of bills tucked in his boot under his bed and he'd miss the satisfaction of adding twenty bucks to it on payday. Tore down the flier in the laundromat so no one else could beat him to it: a '67 Ford Econoline. Needed a new finish, glossy, but the guys on 125th owed him one. And then he'd supplement his Horizon shifts with his own jobs. Weekends, too, bring on Larry so he can pay off his old lady. You couldn't count on the Department of Sanitation, but Larry bellyaching about his child support was as dependable as U.S. Steel.

He decided to call his company Ace Moving. AAA was taken and he wanted to be at the top of the phone book. It was six months before he realized he picked the name from his time at Nickel. Ace: out in the free world to make your zigzag way.

CHAPTER TWELVE

There were four ways out of Nickel.

One: Serve your time. A typical sentence fell between six months and two years, but the administration had the power to confer a legal discharge before then at its discretion. Good behavior was a trigger for a legal discharge, if a careful boy gathered enough merits for promotion to Ace. Whereupon he was released into the bosom of his family, who were very glad to have him back or else winced at the sight of his face bobbing up the walk, the start of another countdown to the next calamity. If you had family. If not, the state of Florida's child-welfare apparatus had assorted custodial remedies, some more pleasant than others.

You could also serve time by aging out. The school showed boys the door on their eighteenth birthday, quick handshake and pocket change. Free to return home or to make their way in the indifferent world, likely shunted down one of life's more difficult trails. Boys arrived banged up in different ways before they got to Nickel and picked up more dents and damage during their term. Often graver missteps and more fierce institutions waited. Nickel boys were fucked before, during, and after their time at the school, if one were to characterize the general trajectory.

Two: The court might intervene. That magic event. A long-lost aunt or older cousin materialized to relieve the state of your wardship. The lawyer retained by dear mom, if she had the means, argued mercy on account of changed circumstance: *Now that his father's gone, we need a breadwinner in the house.* Perhaps the judge in charge—a new one or the same sourpuss—stepped in for his own reasons. Like, money changed hands. But if there had been bribe money, the boy wouldn't have been cast into Nickel in the first place. Still, the law was corrupt and capricious in various measure and sometimes a boy strolled out through what passed for divine intervention.

Three: You could die. Of "natural causes" even, if abetted by unhealthy conditions, malnutrition, and the pitiless constellation of negligence. In the summer of 1945, one young boy died of heart failure while locked in a sweatbox, a popular corrective at that time, and the medical examiner called it natural causes. Imagine baking in one of those iron boxes until your body gave out, wrung. Influenza, tuberculosis, and pneumonia killed their share, as did accidents, drownings, and falls. The fire of 1921 claimed twenty-three lives. Half the dormitory exits were bolted shut and the two boys in the dark third-floor cells were prevented from escaping.

The dead boys were put in the dirt of Boot Hill or released into the care of their family. Some deaths were more nefarious than others. Check the school records, incomplete as they may be. Blunt trauma, shotgun blast. In the first half of the twentieth century, boys who had been leased out to local families wound up dead sometimes. Students were killed while on "unauthorized leave." Two boys were run over by trucks. These deaths were never investigated. The archaeologists at the University of South Florida noticed that the death rates of those who attempted multiple escapes were higher than those who did not. One speculates. As for the unmarked graveyard, it kept its secrets close.

Fourth: Finally, you could run. Make a run for it and see what happened.

Some boys escaped into silent futures under different names in different places, living in shadow. Dreading for the rest of their lives the day Nickel caught up with them. Most often runners were captured, taken for a tour of the Ice Cream Factory, and then ushered into a dark cell for a couple of weeks of attitude adjustment. It was crazy to run and crazy not to run. How could a boy look past the school's property line, see that free and living world beyond, and not contemplate a dash to freedom? To write one's own story for once. To forbid the thought of escape, even that slightest butterfly thought of escape, was to murder one's humanity.

One famous Nickel escapee was Clayton Smith. His story wending its way through the years. The supervisors and housemen made sure of its longevity.

It was 1952. Clayton was not the most likely runaway. Not bright or hale, defiant or spirited. He simply lacked the will to endure. Ground down plenty before he stepped on campus, but Nickel magnified and refined the cruelty of the world, opening his eyes to the bleaker wavelengths. If he'd suffered all this in his fifteen years, what more lay in store?

The men in Clayton's family shared a strong family resemblance. Neighborhood folks recognized them immediately from their hawkish profiles, light brown eyes, the flittering way they moved their hands and mouths when they talked. The similarities persisted beneath the skin, for Smith men were neither lucky nor long-lived. With Clayton there was no mistaking the resemblance.

Clayton's daddy had a heart attack when the boy was four years old. His hand a claw on the bedsheets, mouth wide, eyes wide. At ten, Clayton left school to work in the Manchester orange groves, following his three brothers and two sisters. The baby of the family, pitching in. His mama's health failed after a bout of pneumonia and the state of Florida assumed guardianship. Scattered the children. In Tampa, they still called Nickel the Florida Industrial School for Boys. It had a reputation for improving a young man's character, whether he was a bad seed or simply had no other place to go. His older sisters wrote him letters that his fellow students read to him. His brothers went this way and that, swept up.

Clayton had never learned to fight, not with older siblings around to cow the bullies. At Nickel he fared poorly in the skirmishes. The only time he felt good and level was when he worked in the kitchen, peeling potatoes. It was quiet then and he had a system. The house father of Roosevelt at that time was named Freddie Rich, and his employment history was a map of helpless children. Mark G. Giddins House, the Gardenville School for Young Men, St. Vincent Orphanage over in Clearwater. The Nickel Academy for Boys. Freddie Rich identified candidates by their gait and posture, administration files strengthened the argument, and their treatment by the other boys provided final confirmation. He made quick work of young Clayton, his fingers finding two vertebrae that told the boy, *Now.*

Freddie Rich's quarters were up on Roosevelt's third floor, but he preferred to take his prey to the basement of the white schoolhouse in keeping with Nickel tradition. After that last trip to Lovers' Lane, Clayton was done. The two supervisors who caught him crossing campus that night were accustomed to seeing the boy walking back to the dormitory unescorted. They let him pass. He had a head start.

The boy's plan involved his sister Bell, who'd landed at a home for girls on the outskirts of Gainesville. In contrast with the rest of the family, she enjoyed improved circumstances. The people who ran the home were a kindly sort, enlightened when it came to racial matters. No more corn mash and frayed dresses. She was back in school and only worked on weekends, when she and the other girls took in mending. When she was old enough, she wrote Clayton, she'd come for him and they'd be together again. Bell had dressed and bathed him when he was little and all notions of comfort in his life were an allusion to those early, half-remembered days. The night of his escape he got to the rim of the swamp, where common sense told him to enter the dark water, but he couldn't bring himself to do it. Too forbidding, between the phantoms, murk, and animal symphony of sex and aggression. The dark had always terrified Clayton and only Bell knew the songs that soothed him, cradling his head in her lap as he wound her braids in his fingers. He headed east to the edges of the lime fields until he got to Jordan Road.

He crept in the woods along the road through first light and into the afternoon. Every car sent him into the burrs and underbrush. When he couldn't take another step he hid under a lonesome gray house and squatted in the fetid water of the crawl space. Bugs made supper of him and he caressed the bumps on his skin to see how much he could soothe them without scratching open the bites. The family returned home, a mother and father and teenage girl whom he only saw the feet and knees of. The girl was pregnant, he learned, and this had upturned the order. Or the house had always been a storm and this was the same weather. He slithered forth when the bickering stopped and they slept.

The side of the road was gloomy and fearsome and the boy had no idea about the direction of his travel, but he was unconcerned. Long as he didn't hear hunting dogs, he was okay. As it happened, the Apalachee hounds were deployed elsewhere, attending to the escape of three Piedmont convicts, and Freddie Rich didn't report Clayton's disappearance for twenty-four hours, scared as a trapped rat that his predations would be uncovered. He'd been dismissed from previous jobs and he liked the easy bounty of his latest post.

Had Clayton ever been alone? In the house on that dead-end street in Tampa, his brothers and sisters were ever on top of him, all of them crammed into the three rooms of the rickety shotgun. Then Nickel with its communal debasements. He wasn't accustomed to so much time with the knocking of his thoughts, which rattled around his skull like dice. He hadn't thought of a future beyond a reunion with his family. On the third day, he concocted a scenario—a couple of years as a cook, then saving up for his own restaurant.

Soon after Clayton started picking at the orange groves, Chet's Drive-In opened up on a broken stretch of county road. He looked through the slats of the truck on the way to work, waiting for that red, white, and blue explosion of the restaurant's facade and steel canopy. They hung the banners, the signs sprouted along the road to tease, and then it opened: Chet's. The young white waiters and waitresses wore smart green-and-white striped jumpsuits and smiled as they ferried burgers and shakes out to the lot. The slick jumpsuits encoded virtues—industry, self-reliance. Those fancy cars and the hands sticking out to receive. It was inspiring.

True, Clayton had never eaten in a restaurant and over-esteemed the grandeur of the joint. And perhaps his hunger nourished the idea of owning a dining establishment. As he ran, the vision of his restaurant—walking among the customers to ask how they enjoyed the meal, checking the day's receipts in the back office like he'd seen in movies—kept pace with him.

On the fourth day he was far enough that he decided to hitch. His Nickel dungarees and work shirt were a sight. He swiped work clothes from a clothesline after he saw a battered pickup grind away from a big white farmhouse. He cased the house for a spell and snatched overalls and a shirt when he thought it was safe. An old woman on the second floor watched him lope out of the woods and grab them. The work clothes had been her late husband's and repurposed by her grandson. She was glad to watch them go because it pained her to see them on another person, especially her son's boy, who was cruel to animals and a blasphemer.

He didn't care where his ride was headed as long as it took him a couple of hours' distance. Clayton was starving. He'd never gone this long without eating and didn't know how to remedy that, but miles were the most important thing. Not many cars passed and the white faces scared him, even if he was bold enough to take to the asphalt. There were no Negro drivers; maybe Negroes didn't own cars in this part of the state. He finally forced himself to stick out his thumb when a white Packard with midnight blue trim rounded the bend. He couldn't see the driver but Packards were the first cars he learned to recognize and he had a fondness for them.

The driver was a middle-aged white man in a cream-colored suit. Of course it was a white man, how could it be otherwise in that car? He wore his blond hair parted and had silver squares of hair at the temples. His eyes changed from blue to ice-white behind his wire-frame eyeglasses, depending on the sun.

The man looked Clayton up and down. He beckoned the boy inside. "Where you headed, boy?"

Clayton said the first thing that popped into his head: "Richards." The name of the street he grew up on.

"I don't know it," the white man said. He mentioned a town Clayton had never heard of and said that he'd take him as far as he was going.

Clayton had never been in a Packard before. He rubbed the fabric next to his right thigh, where the man couldn't see: It was rippled and yielding. He wondered after the maze of pistons and valves under the hood, what it'd be like to see how the good men at the plant had put it together.

"You live there, boy?" the man asked. "Richards?" He sounded educated.

"Yes, sir. With my mama and daddy."

"Okay," the man said. "What's your name, boy?"

"Harry," Clayton said.

"You can call me Mr. Simmons." Nodding as if they had an understanding.

They drove for a while. Clayton wasn't going to speak unless spoken to and kept his lips squished to keep something stupid from flying out. Now that it wasn't his two dumb feet moving him, he got agitated and scanned for police cars. Rebuked himself for not staying out of sight longer. He pictured Freddie Rich at the head of the posse, holding a flashlight, the sun gleaming off the big buffalo belt buckle Clayton knew so well—the sight of it, the clatter of it on the concrete floor. The houses got closer together and the Packard eased through a short main street, the boy sinking in his seat but trying not to let the man notice. Then they were on a quiet road once more.

"How old are you?" Mr. Simmons asked. They had just passed a closed-down Esso station, the pumps rusted to scarecrows, and a white church next to a small graveyard. The ground had settled, sending the tombstones off-kilter so that the graveyard was a mouthful of rotten teeth.

"Fifteen," Clayton said. He realized who the man reminded him of—Mr. Lewis, their old landlord. Best pay him on the first of the month or you're out on the street on the second. He got a queasy feeling. The boy made a fist. He knew what he'd do if the man put his hand on his leg or tried to touch his thing. He'd vowed to sock Freddie Rich in the face many times and then stood paralyzed when the time came, but this day he felt he could actually do it. Drawing strength from the free world.

"You in school, boy?"

"Yes, sir." It was a Tuesday, he was pretty sure. He counted back. Freddie Rich liked to look him up Saturday nights. *Cheaper than a dime-a-dance and you get more for your money.*

"An education is important," Mr. Simmons said. "It opens doors. Especially for your people." The moment passed. Clayton spread his fingers on the upholstery as if palming a basketball.

How many days before he got to Gainesville? He remembered the name of Bell's home—Miss Mary's—but he'd have to ask around. What kind of city was Gainesville? There was a lot of this plan he had to figure out before he set things up for himself. Bell would devise secret signals and places to meet that only she knew about. She was smart that way. It'd be a long time before she tucked him in again and told him the things that made it all fine, but he could wait it out if she was close. "Hush now, Clayton . . ."

That's what he was thinking when the Packard rolled past the stone columns at the foot of the Nickel driveway. Mr. Simmons had just retired as the mayor of Eleanor, but he remained a member of the board and kept abreast of the life of the school. Three white students on the way to the metal shop saw Clayton get out of the car but didn't know that he was the boy who ran away, and at midnight the fan bellowed its news to the half asleep but that didn't tell them who was getting ice cream, and in those days the boys didn't know that cars heading out to the school dump in the middle of the night meant that the secret graveyard had welcomed a new resident. It took Freddie Rich to bring Clayton Smith's story to the student population, when he gave it to his latest boy as an object lesson.

You could run and hope to get away. Some made it. Most didn't.

There was a fifth way out of Nickel, according to Elwood. He cooked it up after his grandmother came on visiting day. It was a warm February afternoon, and the families gathered at the picnic tables outside the dining hall. Some boys were local and their mothers and fathers appeared every weekend with sacks of food, new socks, and news from the neighborhood. But the students came from all over the state, Pensacola to the Keys, and most families had far to travel if they wanted to see their wayward sons. Long trips on stuffy buses, warm juice and sandwich crumbs tumbling from wax paper onto laps. Work intervened, distance made visits impossible, and there were some boys who understood that their families had washed their hands of them. On visiting day, after services, the housemen informed the boys whether or not anyone was coming up the hill, and if no one was coming, the boys busied themselves on the playing fields, or found distraction in the tables of the woodshop or in the swimming pool—white kids in the morning, colored kids in the afternoon—and averted their eyes from the reunions up the hill.

Harriet made the trip to Eleanor twice a month but had missed her last visit because of sickness. She sent a letter telling Elwood it was a chest cold and included some newspaper articles she thought he'd like, an account of a Martin Luther King speech in Newark, New Jersey, and a big color spread on the space race. She looked years older, walking slowly toward him. Her illness had stolen from her already slight frame, her collarbones tracing a line across her green dress. When she spotted Elwood, she halted and let him come close for an embrace. It bought her a moment of rest before the final steps to the picnic table he'd staked out.

Elwood held her longer than usual, nuzzling into her shoulder. Then he remembered the other boys and withdrew. Best not to show too much of himself. It had been a long wait for her return, and not just because she had promised some good news the next time she came from Tallahassee.

His life at Nickel had slowed to an obedient shuffle. The period after New Year's was unremarkable. The Eleanor deliveries cycled through the regulars a few times, and Elwood knew what to expect at each stop, even reminding Harper more than once that this Wednesday was the Top Shop and the restaurant beat, like he'd helped out Mr. Marconi back in the tobacco shop. The dormitories were quieter than they'd been through the fall. Fistfights and scuffles were rare and the White House remained unoccupied. Once it was clear that Earl wasn't going to kick the bucket, Elwood and Turner and Desmond forgave Jaimie. Most afternoons they played Monopoly, their game a conspiracy of house rules, obscure covenants, and revenge. Buttons replaced the lost tokens.

The more routine his days, the more unruly his nights. He woke after midnight, when the dormitory was dead, starting at imagined sounds—footsteps at the threshold, leather slapping the ceiling. He squinted at the darkness—nothing. Then he was up for hours, in a spell, agitated by rickety thoughts and weakened by an ebbing of the spirit. It wasn't Spencer that undid him, or a supervisor or a new antagonist slumbering in room 2, rather it was that he'd stopped fighting. In keeping his head down, in his careful navigation so that he made it to lights-out without mishap, he fooled himself that he had prevailed. That he had outwitted Nickel because he got along and kept out of trouble. In fact he had been ruined. He was like one of those Negroes Dr. King spoke of in his letter from jail, so complacent and sleepy after years of oppression that they had adjusted to it and learned to sleep in it as their only bed.

In less kind moments, he had counted Harriet among their number. Now she looked the part, diminished as much as he was. A wind easing after blustering for as long as you could remember.

"Can we squeeze in with y'all?"

Burt, another boy from Cleveland, one of the chucks, wanted to share the picnic table. Burt's mother thanked them and smiled. She was young, maybe twenty-five years old, with a round, open face. Harried yet graceful as she juggled Burt's baby sister, who squatted in her lap hooting at the bugs. Their goofing and play distracted Elwood as his grandmother spoke. They were loud and happy—Elwood and his grandmother were church-quiet beside them. Burt was a rambunctious kid but sweet-hearted from what Elwood had seen. He didn't know the boy well, or his troubles, but he might straighten up and fly right when he got out. His mother waited for him in the free world and that was mighty. More than most of the boys had.

Elwood's grandmother might not be there when he got out. This had never occurred to him before. She was rarely sick, and when she was, she refused to stay off her feet. She was a survivor but the world took her in bites. Her husband had died young, her daughter had vanished out West, and now her only grandson had been sentenced to this place. She had swallowed the portion of misery the world had given to her, and now there she was, alone on Brevard Street, her family tugged away one by one. She might not be there.

Elwood knew she had bad news because she kept on longer than usual about the goings-on around their corner of Frenchtown. Clarice Jenkins's daughter got into Spelman, Tyrone James was smoking in bed and burned his house down, a new hat store opened up on Macomb. She threw him a bone about the movement: "Lyndon Johnson's carrying on President Kennedy's civil rights bill. Bringing it to Congress. And if that good old boy is doing right, you know things is changing. Be a whole different thing when you come home, Elwood."

"Your thumb's dirty," Burt said, "take it out of your mouth. Here's mine instead." He stuck it at his sister and she grimaced and giggled.

Elwood reached across the table and grabbed Harriet's hands. He'd never touched her like that before, as if reassuring a child. "Grandma, what is it?"

Most visitors wept on visiting day at some point, at the sight of the Nickel turnoff coming up the road, on departure, with their backs to their sons. Burt's mother handed his grandmother a handkerchief. She turned away to wipe her eyes.

Harriet's fingers trembled; he stilled them.

The lawyer was gone, she said. Mr. Andrews, the nice, polite white lawyer who'd been so optimistic about Elwood's appeal, had picked up stakes to Atlanta without a word. And taken two hundred dollars of their money with him. Mr. Marconi had kicked in another hundred after meeting with him, which was out of character, yes, but Mr. Andrews had been adamant and persuasive. What they had on their hands was a classic miscarriage of justice. The lawyer's office was empty when she took the bus downtown to see him, she said. The landlord was showing the office to a prospective renter, a dentist. They looked at her like she was nothing.

"I let you down, El," she said.

"I'm okay," he said. "I just made Explorer." He kept his head down and was rewarded. Just like they wanted.

There were four ways out. In the throes of his next midnight spell Elwood decided there was a fifth way.

Get rid of Nickel.

CHAPTER THIRTEEN

He never missed a marathon. He didn't care for the winners, those Superman types hunting world records, slapping down that New York asphalt over bridges and up the extra-wide borough avenues. Camera crews in cars trailed them, zooming in on every drop of sweat and veins jumping in their necks, and white cops on motorcycles, too, to keep nuts from running out from the sidelines and messing with them. Those guys got enough applause, what did they need him for? The winner last year was this African brother, dude was from Kenya. This year it was a white guy from Britain. Built the same, skin color aside—look at those legs and you know they're going to be in the paper. Pros, training all year, jetting all over the globe to compete. It was easy to root for the winners.

No, he liked the punch-drunk ones, half walking at mile twenty-three, tongues flapping like Labradors. Tumbling across the finish line by hook or by crook, feet pounded to bloody meat in their Nikes. The laggards and limpers who weren't running the course but running deep into their character—down into the cave to return to the light with what they found. By the time they got to Columbus Circle, the TV crews have split, the cone cups of water and

Gatorade litter the course like daisies in a pasture, and the silver space blankets twist in the wind. Maybe they had someone waiting for them and maybe they didn't. Who wouldn't celebrate that?

The winners ran alone at the front, then the race course filled up with the pack, the normal joes crammed together. He came out for the runners bringing up the rear and for the crowds on the sidewalks and street corners, those New York mobs so oddball and lovely that they summoned him from his uptown apartment by a force he could only call kinship. Every November the race pitted his skepticism about human beings against the fact that they were all in this dirty city together, unlikely cousins.

The spectators stood on tippy-toes, bellies rubbing on the blue wooden police barriers that get rolled out for races, riots, and presidents, jostling for sight lines, on the shoulders of daddies and boyfriends. Amid the noise of air horns, wolf whistles, and ghetto blasters shouting out old calypso tunes. "Go!" and "You can do it!" and "You got it!" Depending on the breeze the air smelled of Sabrett hot-dog carts or the hairy armpit of that tank-topped chick adjacent. To think of those Nickel nights where the only sounds were tears and insects, how you could sleep in a room crammed with sixty boys and still understand that you were the only person on earth. Everybody around and nobody around at the same time. Here everybody was around and by some miracle you didn't want to wring their neck but give them a hug. The whole city, poor people and Park Avenue types, black and white, Puerto Ricans, on the curb, holding signs and national flags and cheering the people who had been their opponents the day before in front of them at the A&P

checkout, grabbing the last seat on the subway, walking like a walrus too slow on the sidewalk. Competitors for apartments, for schools, for the very air—all those hard-won and cherished animosities fell away for a few hours as they celebrated a rite of endurance and vicarious suffering. *You can do it.*

Tomorrow it was back to the front but this afternoon the truce held until the last runner's last cheer.

The sun was gone. November decided to remind everybody they lived in its kingdom now, ordering up gusts. He exited the park at Sixty-Sixth, darted between two cops on horses, reflected in the cops' sunglasses as a black minnow. The dispersing spectators thinned when he got off Central Park West.

"Hey, man! Hey, hold up a minute!"

Like many New Yorkers he had a crackhead alert system and turned, steeling himself.

The man grinned. "You know me, man—Chickie! Chickie Pete!"

So it was. Chickie Pete from Cleveland, a man now.

He didn't run into a lot of people from the old days. One of the advantages of living up north. He saw Maxwell one time at a wrestling match at the Garden, Jimmy "Superfly" Snucka in a steel match swooping through the air like a giant bat. Maxwell was in line at one of the concessions, close enough to see the six-inch scar on his forehead that leapt over his eye socket and gouged into his jaw. And he thought he saw pigeon-toed Birdy once outside Gristedes, had that same curly golden hair, but the guy looked straight through him. As if he were in disguise, crossing the border under false documents.

"How you doing, man?" His old Nickel comrade wore a green Jets sweatshirt and red track pants that were a size too big, borrowed.

"Hanging in there. You look good." He'd pegged the energy correctly—Chickie wasn't a crackhead but he'd been around the block a few times, with that too-raw thing druggies have when they just get out of jail or a clinic. Here he was, slapping him five, grabbing his shoulder, and talking too loud in a performance of gregariousness. A walking flinch.

"My man!"

"Chickie Pete."

"Where you headed?" Chickie Pete proposed a beer, drinks on him. He begged off, but Chickie Pete wouldn't hear of it, and after the marathon perhaps a test of goodwill for his fellow man was in order. Even when the fellow man hailed from dark days.

He knew Chipp's from his Eighty-Second Street days, before he moved uptown. Columbus was a sleepy stretch when he came to the city—everything closed by eight, tops—and then neighborhood joints opened up on the avenue, singles bars and restaurants that took reservations. Like everywhere in the city: It's a dump and then presto, it's the in-thing. Chipp's was a proper saloon—bartenders who tracked your usual, decent burgers, conversation if you want it and a nod if you don't. The only time he remembered something racial happening, this cracker in a Red Sox cap started going *nigger this* and *nigger that* and got kicked out in a hot minute.

Horizon guys liked to duck in on Mondays and Thursdays, Annie's shifts, on account of her buy-back policy and her bosom, both generous. After he got Ace up and running, he sometimes took his employees out and brought them here, until he learned that if he drank with the guys they took liberties. Show up late or no-show with lame excuses. Or scruffy, their uniforms rumpled. He paid good money for those uniforms. Designed the logo himself.

The game was on, sound low. He and Chickie sat at the bar and the bartender placed their pints on coasters advertising Smiles, a fern bar that used to be a few blocks up the street. The bartender was new, a white guy. A redhead with a bumpkin manner. He liked to pump iron, his T-shirt sleeves as tight as a rubber on his biceps. The kind of gorilla you hire for Saturday nights if you get a crowd.

He put down a twenty even though Chickie said drinks were on him. "You used to play trumpet," he said. Chickie was in the colored band and made a splash in the New Year's talent show with a jazzy version of "Greensleeves," if he recalled, a rendition that verged on bebop.

Chickie smiled at the reminder of his talent. "That was a long time ago. My hands." He held up two fingers that curled like crab legs. He said he'd just spent thirty days drying out.

Mentioning that they sat in a bar seemed impolite.

But Chickie had always made accommodations with his shortcomings. The boy had been a reedy little runt when he got to Nickel and regularly punked out his first year until he learned to fight, and then he preyed on the smaller kids, taking them into closets and supply rooms—you teach what you're taught. That, and the trumpet thing was all he remembered about the Nickel Boy, before Chickie started into his life after graduation. It was a familiar tune, one he'd heard over the years—not from Nickel Boys but from dudes who spent time in similar places. A stint in the army, the routine and discipline appealed to him. "A lot of guys went from juvie into the armed forces. It's like a natural option, especially if you got no home to go back to. Or want to go back to." Chickie was in the military for twelve years, and then he had a crack-up and they drummed him out. Married a couple of times. Any job he could get. The best was selling stereos in Baltimore. He could go on forever about hi-fis.

"I always drank," Chickie said. "Then it was like the more I tried to settle down, the more I got fucked up every night."

Last May he beat up a guy in a bar. The judge said it was either jail or a program, no choice at all. He was in town visiting his sister, who lived in Harlem. "She letting me stay while I figure out my next move. I've always liked it up here."

Chickie asked him what he was up to, and Elwood felt bad telling him about his company so he cut the number of trucks and employees by half and didn't mention the new office on Lenox, which he was quite proud of. Ten-year lease. The longest thing he'd ever committed to, and it was weird because the only thing that bothered him about it was that he wasn't bothered about it.

"My man," Chickie said. "Moving on up! Got a lady?"

"Never settled down, I guess. I go out, when work ain't so bad."

"I hear you, I hear you."

The light from the street dropped a shade as the taller buildings ushered a premature evening. It was the cue for a dose of the Sunday-night back-to-work blues, and he wasn't the only one afflicted—there was a rush at the bar. The muscle-bound bartender served the two blond coeds first, underage probably and testing alcohol enforcement south of their Columbia University stomping grounds. Chickie ordered another beer, outpacing him.

They started in on the old days, quickly sliding to the dark stuff, the worst of the housemen and supervisors. Didn't say Spencer's name, as if it might conjure him on Columbus Avenue like a peckerwood specter, that childhood fear still kept close. Chickie mentioned the Nickel Boys he ran into over the years—Sammy, Nelson, Lonnie. This one was a crook, that one lost an arm in Vietnam, another one was strung out. Chickie said the names of guys he hadn't thought of in forever, it was like a picture of the Last Supper, twelve losers with Chickie in the middle. That's what the school did to a boy. It didn't stop when you got out. Bend you all kind of ways until you were unfit for straight life, good and twisted by the time you left.

Where did that leave him. How bent was he?

"You got out in '64?" Chickie asked.

"You don't remember?"

"What?"

"Nothing. Time served"—a lie told many times, when he slipped up and mentioned reform school—"and they kicked me out. Went up to Atlanta and then kept going north. You know. I've been here since '68. Twenty years." All this time he'd taken it as a given that his escape was a Nickel legend. The students passing his story around as if he were a folk hero, a Stagger Lee figure scaled down to teenage size. But it hadn't happened. Chickie Pete didn't even recall how he got out. If he wanted to be remembered, he should have carved his name into a pew like everyone else. He lit another cigarette.

Chickie Pete squinted. "Hey, hey, what happened to that kid you used to hang around with all the time?"

"Which guy?"

"The guy with that thing. I'm trying to remember."

"Hmm."

"It'll come back to me," he said, and split to the bathroom. He made a remark to a table of gals celebrating a birthday. They laughed at him when he went into the men's room.

Chickie Pete and his trumpet. He might have played professionally, why not? A session man in a funk band, or an orchestra. If things had been different. The boys could have been many things had they not been ruined by that place. Doctors who cure diseases or perform brain surgery, inventing shit that saves lives. Run for president. All those lost geniuses—sure not all of them were geniuses, Chickie Pete for example was not solving special relativity—but they had been denied even the simple pleasure of being ordinary. Hobbled and handicapped before the race even began, never figuring out how to be normal.

The tablecloths were new since the last time he was here—red-and-white checkered vinyl. Denise used to complain about the sticky tables, in those days. Denise—that was one thing he'd messed up. Around him the civilians ate their cheeseburgers and drank their pints, in their free-world cheer. An ambulance sped by outside and in the dark mirror behind the liquor he had a vision of himself outlined a bright red, a shimmering aura that marked him as an outsider. Everybody saw it, just like he knew Chickie's story in two notes. They'd always be on the lam, no matter how they got out of that school.

No one in his life stayed long.

Chickie Pete slapped him on the back on his return. He got mad suddenly, thinking about how knuckleheads like Chickie were still breathing and his friend wasn't. He stood. "I got to go, man."

"No, no, I hear you. Me, too," Chickie said, with the surety of those who have nothing to do. "I don't want to ask," Chickie said.

Here it comes.

"But if you're looking for a hand, I could use the job. I'm sleeping on a couch."

"Right."

"You have a card?"

He started for his wallet and his ACE MOVING business cards—"Mr. Elwood Curtis, President"—but thought better of it. "Not on me."

"I can handle the work, is what I'm putting out there." Chickie wrote his sister's number on a red bar napkin. "You ring me up—for the old days."

"I will."

Once he made sure Chickie Pete was good and gone, he headed for Broadway. He had the uncharacteristic urge to take the bus, the 104 up Broadway. Take the scenic route and absorb the life of the city. He nixed it: The marathon was over, and his feeling of bonhomie was as well. In Brooklyn and Queens and the Bronx and Manhattan, the cars and trucks had resumed ownership of the blocked-off streets, the marathon route disappeared mile by mile. Blue paint on asphalt marked the course—every year it flaked away before you knew it. The white plastic bags skittering down the block and the overflowing trash cans were back, the McDonald's wrappers and red-top crack vials crunching underfoot. He grabbed a cab and thought about dinner.

It was funny, how much he had liked the idea of his Great Escape making the rounds of the school. Pissing off the staff when they heard the boys talking about it. He thought this city was a good place for him because nobody knew him—and he liked the contradiction that the one place that *did* know him was the one place he didn't want to be. It tied him to all those other people who come to New York, running away from hometowns and worse. But even Nickel had forgotten his story.

Knocking Chickie for being a fuckup when he was going home to his empty apartment.

He ripped up Chickie Pete's red napkin and tossed it out the window. *No One Likes a Litterbug* popped into his head, courtesy of the city's new quality-of-life drive. A successful campaign, judging from the way it stayed with him. "So give me a ticket," he said.

CHAPTER FOURTEEN

Director Hardee suspended two days of classes to get the facility in shape for the state inspection. It was a surprise inspection, but his fraternity brother ran child welfare down in Tallahassee and made a phone call. Plenty of long-standing cosmetic items required attention despite the students' work details. The sun-cracked basketball court called for a new surface and hoops, and rust afflicted the tractors and harrows on the farms. An alien light radiated when the boys wiped generations of grime from the skylights in the printing plant. Most of the buildings, from the hospital to the schoolhouses to the garages, badly needed a new coat of paint, the dormitories—especially those for colored students—most of all. It was quite a sight, all the boys, big and small, hustling in unified purpose, paint on their chins, the chucks wobbling as they ferried the cans of Dixie across campus.

At Cleveland, Carter the houseman drew upon his construction days and demonstrated how to tuck-point the cracks between those good Nickel bricks. Crowbars wrenched the rotten floorboards; new ones were cut and set. Hardee called in outsiders for the specialty work. The new boiler, delivered two years earlier, was finally installed.

Plumbers replaced two broken urinals on the second floor, and burly roofers took care of blisters and punctures up top. No more early-morning leaks waking the boys of room 2.

The White House got a new coat. No one saw who did it. One day it was its dingy self, the next it made the sun vibrate on eyeballs.

Judging from Hardee's face as he toured the progress, the boys were on track for a good showing. Every few decades a newspaper report about embezzlement or physical abuse at the school initiated an investigation by the state. In their wake came prohibitions against "spanking," and the use of dark cells and sweatboxes. The administration instituted a stricter accounting of school supplies, which had a tendency to disappear, as well as the profits from the various student businesses, which also liked to disappear. The parole of students to local families and businesses was terminated and the medical staff increased. They fired the longtime dentist and found one who didn't charge by the extraction.

It had been years since there were any allegations against Nickel. On this occasion the school was merely another item on a long list of government facilities due a once-over.

Work assignments—farming, printing, brick-making, and the like—continued as usual, because they promoted responsibility, built character, etc., and were an important source of revenue. Two days before the inspection, Harper dropped off Elwood and Turner at the house of Mr. Edward Childs, a former county supervisor and longtime booster of the Nickel Academy for Boys. The school and the family went back a ways. Edward Childs and the Kiwanis Club had gone fifty-fifty on the football uniforms five years earlier. It was hoped that he'd repeat his generosity, given an incentive.

Mr. Childs's father, Bertram, had served in local government and had also sat on the school board. He was an avid proponent of peonage, back when it was allowed, and often leased paroled students. They tended the horses when there had been a stable out back, and the chickens. The basement that Elwood and Turner cleaned out that afternoon had been where the indentured boys slept. When the moon was full, the boys had stood on the cot and gazed upon its milky eye through the single cracked window.

Elwood and Turner were unaware of the basement's history. They were charged with removing sixty years of junk so that it could be converted into a rec room, with checkerboard floor tile and wood paneling. The Childs's teenagers had been lobbying and Edward Childs was not without his own ideas for the space, as his wife and kids visited her family for two weeks every August and he was left to his own devices. Wet bar over there, install some modern lighting, things they'd seen in magazines. Before those dreams were realized, old bicycles, ancient steamer trunks, broken-down spinning wheels, and a multitude of other dusty relics waited for their final reward. The boys opened the heavy cellar doors and got to work. Harper sat in the van, smoking and listening to the baseball game.

"Junkman's going to love us," Turner said.

Elwood carried a stack of dusty *Saturday Evening Posts* up the stairs and added it to the pile of *Imperial Nighthawks* by the curb. The *Imperial* was a Klan paper; the issue on top featured a black-robed night rider carrying a burning cross. Had Elwood cut the twine, he would have discovered that this was a popular cover theme. He turned over the bundle to hide the image and revealed an ad for Clementine Shaving Cream.

While Turner made jokes under his breath and whistled Martha and the Vandellas, Elwood's thoughts traced a groove. Different newspapers for different countries. He remembered looking up *agape* in his encyclopedia volume after he read Dr. King's speech in the *Defender*. The newspaper ran the address in full after the reverend's appearance at Cornell College. If Elwood had come across the word before, through all those years of skipping around the book, it hadn't stuck in his head. King described *agape* as a divine love operating in the heart of man. A selfless love, an incandescent love, the highest there is. He called upon his Negro audience to cultivate that pure love for their oppressors, that it might carry them to the other side of the struggle.

Elwood tried to get his head around it, now that it was no longer the abstraction floating in his head last spring. It was real now.

Throw us in jail, and we will still love you. Bomb our homes and threaten our children, and, as difficult as it is, we will still love you. Send your hooded perpetrators of violence into our communities after midnight hours, and drag us out onto some wayside road, and beat us and leave us half-dead, and we will still love you. But be ye assured that we will wear you down by our capacity to suffer, and one day we will win our freedom.

The capacity to suffer. Elwood—all the Nickel boys—existed in the capacity. Breathed in it, ate in it, dreamed in it. That was their lives now. Otherwise they would have perished. The beatings, the rapes, the unrelenting winnowing of themselves. They endured. But to love those who would have destroyed them? To make that leap? *We will meet your physical force with soul force. Do to us what you will and we will still love you.*

Elwood shook his head. What a thing to ask. What an impossible thing.

"You hear me?" Turner asked. Wiggling his fingers in Elwood's blank face.

"What?"

Turner needed a hand inside. They'd made good progress, even with Turner's standard delaying technique, unearthing a stash of old steamer trunks beneath the stairs. Silverfish and centipedes made a break for it as the boys dragged the trunks to the center of the basement. The stamps decorating the scruffy black canvas commemorated trips to Dublin, Niagara Falls, San Francisco, and other distant ports of call. A story of exotic travel in bygone days, places these boys would never see in their lives.

Turner huffed. "What's in these things?"

"I've been writing everything down," Elwood said.

"Everything what?"

"The deliveries. The yard work and chores. The names of everybody and the dates. All our Community Service."

"Nigger, why would you do a thing like that?" Knowing why but curious as to how his friend would phrase it.

"You told me. No one else can get me out of here, just me."

"Nobody ever listens to me—why you got to start?"

"I didn't know why I did it at first. That first day with Harper, I wrote down what I saw. And I kept doing it. In one of the school notebooks. It made me feel better. I suppose it was to tell someone someday, and now I'm going to do it. I'm going to give it to the inspectors when they come."

"What do you think they going to do? Put your picture on the cover of *Time* magazine?"

"I did it to stop it."

"Another one of these dummies." Feet thumped over their heads—they never did see the Childs family that entire day—and Turner busied himself like they had X-ray vision. "You're getting along. Ain't had trouble since that one time. They going to take you out back, bury your ass, then they take me out back, too. The fuck is wrong with you?"

"You're wrong, Turner." Elwood tugged on the handle of a weathered brown trunk. It broke in half. "It's not an obstacle course," he said. "You can't go around it—you have to go through it. Walk with your head up no matter what they throw at you."

"I vouched for you," Turner said, wiping his hands on his trousers. "You got ticked off and need to get it off your chest, that's cool." Marking the end of the conversation.

When they were done hauling, the boys had performed surgery—cut the rotten tissue from the house and plopped it on the tray of the curb. Turner banged on the van door to wake Harper. The radio relayed a sizzle of static.

"What's wrong with him?" Harper asked Elwood. Turner was mum, a conspicuous turn.

Elwood shook his head and looked out the window.

His thoughts prowled and roved after midnight. Turner's angry question joined his host of worry. It wasn't, what did he think the white men were going to do but did he trust them to do it?

He was alone in this particular protest. He wrote *The Chicago Defender* twice, but hadn't heard back, even when he mentioned the editorial he'd written under another name. It had been two weeks. More distressing than the notion that the newspaper didn't care about what was going on at Nickel was that they received so many letters like it, so many appeals, that they couldn't address them all. The country was big, and its appetite for prejudice and depredation limitless, how could they keep up with the host of injustices, big and small. This was just one place. A lunch counter in New Orleans, a public pool in Baltimore that they filled with concrete rather than allow black kids to dip a toe in it. This was one place, but if there was one, there were hundreds, hundreds of Nickels and White Houses scattered across the land like pain factories.

If he asked his grandmother to send the letter, avoiding the matter of whether his mail made it out, she'd open it lickety-split and throw it in the trash. Fearful of what would happen to him—and she didn't even know what they'd done to him so far. He had to trust a stranger to do the right thing. It was impossible, like loving the one who wanted to destroy you, but that was the message of the movement: to trust in the ultimate decency that lived in every human heart.

This or this. This world whose injustices have sent you meek and shuffling, or this truer, biding world waiting for you to catch up?

At breakfast the morning of the state visit, Blakeley and the other house fathers of the north campus made clear their message of the day: "You boys mess up, it's your ass." Blakeley, Terrance Crowe from Lincoln, and Freddie Rich, who looked after the boys in Roosevelt. Every day he wore the same buffalo belt buckle, nestled above his crotch and under his potbelly like an animal wending between hills.

Blakeley gave the boys the schedule of the inspection. He was alert and awake, having forsworn his nightcaps. The black boys weren't on display until the afternoon, he said. The inspection commenced with the white campus, the schoolhouse and dormitories, and the big facilities like the hospital and the gymnasium. Hardee wanted to show off the athletic fields and the new basketball court, so that was next before the men from Tallahassee went over the hill to the farms, the printing press, and the renowned Nickel brick plant. Last came the colored campus. "You know Mr. Spencer will have a word for you if he catches you with your shirt untucked or your dirty drawers hanging out of your footlocker," Blakeley said. "And it will not be kind."

The three house fathers stood before the serving trays, which that day were filled with the food the students were supposed to get every morning: scrambled eggs, ham, fresh juice, and pears.

"When they getting here, sir?" one of the chucks asked Terrance. Terrance was a big strapping man with a scraggly white beard and watery eyes. He'd worked at Nickel for more than twenty years, which meant he'd seen different kinds of meanness. Which made him one of the bigger accomplices, in Elwood's estimation.

"Any minute," Terrance said.

When the house fathers took their seats, the boys were permitted to eat.

Desmond looked up from his plate. "I haven't eaten this good since . . ." He couldn't think of it. "They should inspect this place all the time."

"Nobody talking now," Jaimie said. "Eat."

The students dug in happily, scraping plates. The bribe did its job, despite the stern words. The boys were in a pleasant mood, between the grub, the new clothes, the repainted dining hall. Those ragged at the cuff or knee had been given new trousers. Their shoes gleamed. The line outside the barber's had wrapped around the building twice. The students looked smart. Even the ringworm kids.

Elwood searched for Turner. He sat with some Roosevelt boys he bunked with during his first term. From his fake smile, he knew Elwood was looking at him. Turner had barely spoken to Elwood since the day in the basement. He still hung out with Jaimie and Desmond, slinking off when Elwood appeared. He'd been scarce in the rec room and Elwood assumed he was hanging out in his loft. The boy was almost as good as Harriet at the silent treatment, especially given the years of practice his grandmother had on him. This silence's lesson? Keep your mouth shut.

Ordinarily, Wednesdays were Community Service, but for obvious reasons Elwood and Turner were reassigned. Harper grabbed them after breakfast and told them to join the bleacher team. The football bleachers were a splintery mess, wobbly, unsound. Hardee saved their refurbishment for the day of the inspection, as if such large undertakings were just another day at the school. Ten boys were dispatched to sand, replace, and paint the planks on one side of the field, and another ten took care of the bleachers opposite. By the time the inspectors finished with the white campus, the teams would have a nice performance under way. Elwood and Turner were on different teams.

Elwood took to reconnoitering spent or rotten planks. Tiny gray bugs boiled forth and slinked from the daylight. He'd gotten into a nice rhythm when the signal went up—the inspectors had departed the gymnasium and were headed toward the football field. He tried to think of how

Turner would have nicknamed them. The portly one was a ringer for Jackie Gleason, the one with the buzz cut looked like a refugee from Mayberry, and the tall one was JFK. He had the angular WASP features of the dead president and the same splendid white teeth, and had chosen the haircut to heighten the resemblance. Out in the sun, the inspectors took off their suit jackets—it was going to be a humid day—under which they wore the short-sleeve shirts and clipped black ties that made Elwood think of Cape Canaveral and those smart men with impossible trajectories crammed into their skulls.

He lugged his words like an anvil in his Nickel-issued pockets. *Darkness cannot drive out darkness*, the reverend said, *only light can do that. Hate cannot drive out hate, only love can do that.* He'd copied over his list of four months of deliveries and recipients, the names and dates and goods exchanged, the bags of rice and tins of peaches, the sides of beef and Christmas hams. He added three lines about the White House and Black Beauty, and that one of the students, Griff, had gone missing after the boxing championship. All in his finest penmanship. He didn't put his name down, to kid himself that they wouldn't know the author's identity. They'd know he was the snitch, of course, but they'd be in jail.

Is this what it felt like? To walk arm in arm in the middle of the street, a link in a living chain, knowing that around the next corner the white mob stood with their baseball bats and fire hoses and curses. But it was just him, as Turner told him that day in the hospital.

The boys had been trained to wait until spoken to before talking to a white man. Learned this in their earliest days, in school, on the streets and roads of their dusty towns. Had it reinforced at Nickel: You are a colored boy in a white man's world. He'd considered different theaters for his delivery: the schoolhouse, outside the dining hall, the parking lot by the administration building. He never pulled off this particular emancipation play without interruption—Hardee and Spencer, usually Spencer, inevitably bounded out on the boards, ruining the scene. He'd expected the director and superintendent to take the inspectors around, but the state men roamed unescorted. Moseying on the concrete paths, pointing at this or that, conferring. They stopped people for little talks, calling over a white boy who was running to the library, collaring Miss Baker and another female teacher for a chat.

Maybe it was possible.

JFK, Jackie Gleason, and Mayberry dawdled by the new basketball courts—that had been a shrewd maneuver on Hardee's part—and approached the football fields. Harper muttered, "You boys look busy," and waved at the inspectors. He walked the fifty-yard line to the opposite bleachers to give the illusion of noninterference. Elwood descended the bleachers, stepping around Lonnie and Black Mike, who were awkwardly setting a plank of pine into the scaffold. He had the angle right for interception. A quick handoff—and if Harper saw and asks what's in that envelope, he says it's an essay on how civil rights has changed things for the younger generation of colored folks, he'd been working on it for weeks. It sounded like some corny shit Turner would accuse him of.

Elwood was two yards away from the white men. His heart caught. No budging that anvil any farther. He veered over to the lumber pile and put his hands on his knees.

The inspectors proceeded up the hill. Jackie Gleason

made a joke and the other two laughed. They walked past the White House without a glance.

The other students made so much noise when they saw what the kitchen had cooked up for lunch—hamburgers and mashed potatoes and ice cream that would never see the inside of Fisher's Drugs—that Blakeley told them to keep it down. "You want them to think this is some kind of circus we running here?" Elwood's stomach refused the food. He'd fucked it up. Try again in Cleveland, he decided. The rec room, a quick "excuse me sir" in the hallway. Instead of out in the open, in the middle of the green. He'd have cover. Give it to JFK. But what if the inspector opened it right there? Or read it on the walk down the hill, as Hardee and Spencer caught up with them to escort them off the property?

They had whipped Elwood. But he took the whipping and he was still here. There was nothing they could do that white people hadn't done to black people before, were not doing at this moment somewhere in Montgomery and Baton Rouge, in broad daylight on a city street outside Woolworths. Or some anonymous country road with no one to tell the tale. They would whip him, whip him bad, but they couldn't kill him, not if the government knew what was going on here. His mind strayed—and he saw the National Guard drive through the Nickel gate in a convoy of dark green vans, and soldiers jumping out into formation. Maybe the soldiers didn't agree with what they were sent to do, their sympathies lay with the old order instead of what was right, but they had to abide by the laws of the land. Same way they lined up in Little Rock to let the nine Negro children into Central High School, a human wall between the angry whites and the children, between the past and the future. Governor Faubus couldn't do anything about it because it was bigger than Arkansas and its backward wickedness, it was America. A mechanism of justice set in movement by a woman sitting down on a bus where she was told not to sit, a man ordering ham on rye at a forbidden counter. Or a letter of proof.

We must believe in our souls that we are somebody, that we are significant, that we are worthful, and we must walk the streets of life every day with this sense of dignity and this sense of somebody-ness. If he didn't have that, what did he have? Next time, he would not falter.

The bleacher team headed back after lunch. Harper caught his arm. "Hold on a minute, Elwood."

The other boys cut down the slope. "What is it, Mr. Harper?"

"I need you to head up to the farms and find Mr. Gladwell," he said. Mr. Gladwell and his two assistants oversaw all the planting and harvesting at Nickel. Elwood had never talked to him, but everyone knew him from his straw hat and his farmer's tan, which made him look like he swam across the Rio Grande to get here. "Those men from the state aren't going to head up there today," Harper said, "they're going to send some other experts to check out the farms, special. You find him and tell him he can relax."

Elwood turned to where Harper pointed, down the main road where the three inspectors mounted the steps to Cleveland. They went inside. Mr. Gladwell was God knows where up north, with the lime or potato fields, it was acres and acres. The inspectors would be gone by the time he got back.

"I'm liking the painting, Harper—can one of the little kids go?"

"Mr. Harper, *sir*." On campus they had to go by the rules.

"Sir, I'd rather work on the bleachers."

Harper frowned. "Acting crazy today, all of you. You do what I asked you and on Friday it's back to the usual." Harper left Elwood on the dining-hall steps. Last Christmas, he'd stood in the same spot when Desmond told him and Turner about Earl's stomach trouble.

"I'll do it."

It was Turner.

"What's that?"

"That letter you got in your pocket," Turner said. "I'll get it to them, fuck it. Look at you—you look sick."

Elwood searched for a tell. But Turner stood with the con men of the world and the con men never betray the game.

"I said I'll do it, I'll do it. You got someone else?"

Elwood gave it to him and ran north without a word.

It took Elwood an hour to find Mr. Gladwell, who sat in a big rattan chair at the edge of the sweet potato fields. The man stood and squinted at Elwood.

"Say what now? Guess I can smoke," he said, and relit his cigar. He barked at his charges, who had stalled their labor at the sight of the messenger. "That doesn't mean you can quit, now. Get to it!"

Elwood took the long way back, around the trails that circumnavigated Boot Hill and took him past the stables and laundry. He was slow with his steps. He didn't want to know if Turner had been intercepted, or if the boy had ratted on him or simply taken his letter up to his hideout and put a match to it. Whatever waited for him on the other side would still be waiting for him whenever he got there, so he whistled a tune he remembered from when he was little, a blues tune. He didn't recall the words or whether it had been his father or mother who sang it, but he felt good whenever the song snuck up on him, a kind of coolness like the shadow of a cloud out of nowhere, something that broke off something bigger. Yours briefly before it sailed on its way.

Turner brought him to his warehouse loft before supper. Turner had a license to roam, but Elwood didn't, and he shook off a wave of fear. But if he wrote that letter, he was bold enough to enter the warehouse without permission. The hideout was smaller than in his imagination, a cramped recess Turner had chipped out of the Nickel cave—walls made of crates, a dingy army blanket, and a cushion from the rec-room couch. It was not the hideout of a canny operator but the slim refuge of a runaway who had stepped into a doorway to get out of the rain, collar hugged tight.

Turner sat against a box of machine oil and cradled his knees. "I did it," he said. "I put it in a copy of *The Gator*. In the newspaper, like at the bowling alley when Mr. Garfield slipped a payoff to the fucking cops. Ran up to the man's car and said, 'I thought you'd like a copy.' "

"Which one did you give it to?"

"JFK, who else?" In disdain. "You think I gave it to that dude from *The Honeymooners*?"

"Thanks," Elwood said.

"I didn't do shit, El. I delivered the mail, is all." He put out his hand and the boys shook on it.

The kitchen staff brought out the ice cream again that night. The house fathers, and presumably Hardee, were satisfied with how the inspection had gone. At school the next day, and on Community Service that Friday, Elwood waited for the reaction, like he was back at Lincoln High School and waiting for the volcano to bubble and smoke in science class. The National Guard didn't screech into the parking lot, Spencer didn't put his cold hand on his neck and say, "Boy, we have a problem." It didn't happen like that.

It happened as it ever happened. At night, in the dormitories, flashlights crawling over his face when they took him to the White House.

CHAPTER FIFTEEN

She read about the restaurant in the *Daily News* and left the clipping by his side of the bed so he wouldn't miss it. It had been a while since they'd had a night out together. Three months on, his secretary Yvette still left the office early to care for her mother, which had him playing catch-up at the end of every day. Her mother was senile, but they called it dementia now. As for Millie, it was almost March so the annual madness had descended, April 15 coming up and everybody scrambling. "They have a level of denial that is positively insane," his wife said. She usually got home in time for the eleven o'clock news. He'd canceled date night twice already—*date night* was some women's magazine thing now embedded in his vocabulary like a splinter—so Millie was not going to let him miss this one. "Dorothy has been twice and says it's amazing," Millie said.

Dorothy thought a lot of things were amazing, like gospel brunch, *American Idol*, and organizing a petition against that new mosque opening up. He held his tongue.

He left at seven, after taking a crack at decoding the new health plan Yvette had dug up for Ace. It was cheaper but was he getting ripped off in the long run with the co-pay bullshit? This species of paperwork had always confounded and vexed. He'd have Yvette explain it again when she got in the next day.

He got off at the City College stop on Broadway and peeled off up the hill. It was warmer than it was supposed to be for March, but he remembered more than one April blizzard in Manhattan and wasn't ready to call it spring yet. "It happens right after you put your coat away," he said. Millie told him he sounded like some batty hermit who lived in a cave.

Camille's was on the corner of 141st and Amsterdam, the anchor retail of a seven-story tenement. The *Daily News* review described the place as nouveau Southern, "down-home plates with a twist." What was the twist—that it was soul food made by white people? Chitlins with some pale pickled thing on top? A neon Lone Star beer sign blinked in the window and a halo of battered Alabama license plates surrounded the menu by the entrance. He squinted—his eyes weren't what they used to be. Despite the hillbilly warning signs, the food sounded good and not too fussed over, and when he got to the hostess station, most of the patrons inside were neighborhood people. Black people, Latinos who probably worked in the area, for the college. Squares, but their presence vouched.

The hostess was a white girl in a light blue hippie dress, one of that clan. Chinese-character tattoos scrolled up her wiry arms, who knew what they said. She pretended not to see him and he started up a round of "Racism or Bad Service?" He didn't get far into his calculations before she apologized for the wait—the new system was down, she said, frowning at the gray glow on her stand. "Would you like to sit now or wait for the rest of your party?"

Years of habit made him say he'd wait outside and then on the sidewalk came that too-familiar disappointment—Millie had made him quit. He pushed a tablet of nicotine gum out of the foil.

A warm late-winter evening. He didn't think he'd been on this block before. Up on 142nd he recognized a building from an old job, back when he was still on the truck. He still felt the old days in his back sometimes, a twinge and a quiver. This was Hamilton Heights now. The first time one of his dispatchers asked where Hamilton Heights was, he said, "Tell them they're moving to Harlem." But the name persisted and stuck. Real estate agents cooking up new names for old places, or resurrecting old names for old places, meant the neighborhood was turning over. Meant young people, white people are moving back. He can cover office rent and payroll. You want to pay him to move you into Hamilton Heights or Lower Whoville or whatever they come up with, he's glad to help, three-hour minimum.

White flight in reverse. The children and grandchildren of those who'd fled the island years before, fled the riots and the bankrupt city government and the graffiti that spelled out *Go Fuck Yourself* no matter what the letters said. The city was such a dump when he arrived, he didn't blame them. Their racism and fear and disappointment paid for his new life. You want to pay to move to Roslyn, Long Island, Horizon is glad to help, and if he was getting the hourly wage back then and not paying the hourly wage, he was grateful that Mr. Betts paid on time, in cash, off the books. Didn't matter what his name was or where he'd come from.

A *West Side Spirit* stuck out of the garbage can on the corner and he made a note to tell Millie that he wasn't doing the interview. When they were going to bed, or tomorrow, so as not to spoil the evening. A woman in her book club sold ads for the paper and told Millie she'd put his name up for a feature they were running, spotlighting local businesses. "Enterprising Entrepreneurs." He was a natural—a black man who owned his own moving company, employed local people, mentoring.

"I don't mentor anybody," he told Millie. He was in the kitchen, tying a garbage bag into a knot.

"It's a big honor."

"I'm not one of these people who needs everybody's attention," he said.

It was simple—a quick interview and then they'd send a photographer to take some pictures of his new office on 125th Street. Maybe one of him standing in front of the trucks—the big boss, to put it all in perspective. Out of the question. He'd be nice about it, place an ad or two, and that'd be the end of it.

Millie was five minutes late. Unusual for her.

It bugged him. He stepped back, stepped back some more so he saw the building proper and realized he had been here before. Back in the '70s. The restaurant had been a community center or the like, legal aid, a view of the desks so you can see that everybody looks like you. Help you fill out the application for food stamps and other government programs, break down the discouraging bureaucratese, probably run by some former Panthers. He was still working for Horizon so it had to be the '70s. Top floor, middle of summer, and the elevator was out. Humping up all that white-and-black hexagon tile, the steps worn from so many feet that they seemed to smile, a dozen smiles every floor.

Right: The old lady had died. The son hired them to pack everything and take it to his house on Long Island, where they'd bring it to the basement and shove it up cozy between the boiler and the never-touched fishing rods. Where it would remain until the son died and his children didn't know what to do with it and it started all over again. The family had packed up half the old lady's stuff and then given up—you got to know the signs when people got overwhelmed by the enormity of the undertaking. There were still a bunch of images from the afternoon in his memory: up and down the tenement floor; the sweat soaked into their Horizon T-shirts; the jammed-shut windows that corralled the musty smell of isolation and death; the empty cupboards. The bed she died in, stripped to the blue-and-white striped mattress and her stains.

"Are we taking the mattress?"

"We are not taking the mattress."

Lord knows he had a fear in those days of dying like that. No one knows until the stink alarms the neighbors and the irritated super lets the cops in. Irritated until he sees the body and then after that it's all pieced-together biography—he let the mail pile up, one time he cursed out the nice lady next door and vowed to poison her cats. Die alone in one of his old rooms and what's the last thing he thinks of before he kicks the bucket—Nickel. Nickel hunting him to his final moment—a vessel in his brain explodes or his heart flops in his chest—and then beyond, too. Perhaps Nickel was the very afterlife that awaited him, with a White House down the hill and an eternity of oatmeal and the infinite brotherhood of broken boys. He hadn't thought about going out like that in years—he'd packed it up in a box and put it in his basement, next to the boiler and the neglected fishing gear. With the rest of the stuff from the old days. He stopped embroidering that fantasy long ago. Not because he had someone in his life. But because that someone was Millie. She chipped off the bad parts. He hoped he did the same.

He got a feeling—he wanted to buy her flowers, like when he started taking her out. Eight years since he saw her at the Hale House fund-raiser, filling out her raffle tickets in her careful script. Is that what normal husbands do—buy flowers for no reason? All these years out of that school and he still spent a segment of his days trying to decipher the customs of normal people. The ones who had been raised happily, three meals a day and a kiss goodnight, the ones who had no notion of White Houses, Lovers' Lanes, and white county judges who sentenced you to hell.

She was late. If he hurried he could make it to Broadway and buy a cheap bouquet at a Korean deli before she got there.

"What's this for?" she'll ask.

For being the whole free world.

He should have thought of the flowers sooner, at the deli outside the office or when he stepped out of the subway, because right then she said, "There's my handsome husband," and it was date night.

CHAPTER SIXTEEN

Their daddies taught them how to keep a slave in line, passed down this brutal heirloom. Take him away from his family, whip him until all he remembers is the whip, chain him up so all he knows is chains. A term in an iron sweatbox, cooking his brains in the sun, had a way of bringing a buck around, and so did a dark cell, a room aloft in darkness, outside time.

After the Civil War, when a five-dollar fine for a Jim Crow charge—vagrancy, changing employers without permission, "bumptious contact," what have you—swept black men and women up into the maw of debt labor, the white sons remembered the family lore. Dug pits, forged bars, forbid the nourishing face of the sun. The Florida Industrial School for Boys wasn't in operation six months before they converted the third-floor storage closets into solitary confinement. One of the handymen went dorm by dorm, screwing in bolts: there. The dark cells remained in use even after two locked-up boys died in the fire of '21. The sons held the old ways close.

The state outlawed dark cells and sweatboxes in juvenile facilities after World War II. It was a time of high-minded reform all over, even at Nickel. But the rooms waited, blank and still and airless. They waited for wayward boys in need of an attitude adjustment. They wait still, as long as the sons—and the sons of those sons—remember.

Elwood's second White House beating was not as severe as the first. Spencer didn't know what damage the boy's letter had caused—who else had read it, who cared, what sort of repercussions roiled down in the capitol. "Smart nigger," he said. "I don't know where they get these smart niggers." The superintendent was not his usual jolly self. He gave the boy twenty licks then, distracted, handed Black Beauty to Hennepin for the first time. Spencer had hired Hennepin as Earl's replacement, unaware of how perfectly he had chosen. But like seeks like. Hennepin maintained an expression of dull-witted malice most of the time, lumbering across the grounds, but he brightened at opportunities for cruelty, with a leer and gap-toothed grin. Hennepin beat the boy briefly before Spencer stayed his hand. There was no telling what was happening in Tallahassee. They took the boy to the dark cell.

Blakeley's room was to the right at the top of the stairs. Behind the other door lay the small hallway and the three rooms. The rooms had been repainted for the inspection and piles of bedding and surplus mattresses moved inside. The paint hid the initials of the cells' previous inhabitants, the scratches in the darkness over the years. Initials, names, and also a range of cuss words and entreaties. When the doors opened and the scratches were revealed to the boys who had written them, the hieroglyphics did not resemble what they remembered putting into the walls. It was all demonology.

Spencer and Hennepin hauled the sheets and mattresses to the rooms on either side. The room was empty when they shoved Elwood in. The next afternoon a houseman on the day shift gave the boy a bucket for a toilet, but no more. Light strained through the mesh opening at the top of the door, a gray light his eyes eventually became accustomed to. They gave him food when the other boys left for breakfast, one meal a day.

The last three inhabitants of that particular room had come to bad ends. The place was worse luck on top of bad luck, cursed. Rich Baxter was sentenced to the dark cell for fighting back—a white supervisor boxed his ears, and Rich knocked out three of his teeth. He had a solid right hand. Rich spent a month in the room, thinking of the glorious violence he would deliver to the white world when he got out. Mayhem and murder and assault. Wiping his bloody knuckles on his dungarees. Instead he enlisted in the army and died—it was a closed casket—two days before the end of the Korean War. Five years later, Claude Sheppard got sent upstairs for stealing peaches. He was never the same after those weeks in the dark—a boy went in and a man hobbled out. He renounced misbehavior and sought out cures for his pervasive worthlessness, a kind of sad-sack seeker. Claude overdosed on smack in a Chicago flophouse three years later; potter's field keeps him now.

Jack Coker, Elwood Curtis's immediate predecessor, was discovered engaged in homosexual activity with another student, Terry Bonnie. Jack spent his dark time in Cleveland, Terry on the third floor of Roosevelt. Binary stars in cold space. The first thing Jack did when he got out was to smack Terry in the face with a chair. Well, not the first thing. He had to wait until dinnertime. The other boy was a mirror that granted a ruinous glimpse of himself. Jack died on the floor of a juke-joint floor one month before Elwood arrived at Nickel. He misheard a stranger's remark and lashed out. The stranger had a knife.

After a week and a half, Spencer got tired of being afraid—in truth he was afraid much of the time but was unaccustomed to one of his black boys instigating that fear—and paid Elwood a visit. Things were quieting down at the statehouse, Hardee was less distressed. The worst was over. The government had too much power to interfere, was the problem in general. Way he saw it. It got worse every year. Spencer's daddy had been a supervisor on the south campus and got demoted after one of his charges ended up choked to death. Some roughhousing that got out of hand and he was the scapegoat. Money was tight before; it got tighter. Spencer remembered those days still, the pot of canned corn beef and broth stinking up that little kitchen and him and his brothers and sisters lined up with their chipped bowls. His grandfather had worked for the T. M. Madison Coal Company in Spadra, Arkansas, minding nigger convicts. No one from the county, no one from the main office, dared to interfere with the execution of his office—his grandfather was a craftsman and enjoyed the respect of his achievements. It was demeaning, one of Spencer's boys writing a letter on him.

Spencer took Hennepin with him to the third floor. The rest of the dormitory was at breakfast. "You're probably wondering how long we're going to keep you in here," he said. They kicked Elwood a while and Spencer felt better, like a bubble of worry in his chest up and popped.

The worst thing that ever happened to Elwood happened every day: He woke in that room. He would never tell anyone about those days of darkness. Who would come for him?

He had never considered himself an orphan. He had to stay behind so that his mother and father could find what they needed in California. No point having sad feelings about it—one thing had to happen for the other thing to happen. He had an idea that one day he'd tell his father about his letter, how it was just like the letter his father gave to his commanding officer about the treatment of colored troops, the one that got him a commendation in the war. But he was as much an orphan as many of the boys in Nickel. No one was coming.

He thought long on Dr. Martin Luther King Jr.'s letter from the Birmingham jail, and the powerful appeal the man composed from inside. One thing gave birth to the other—without the cell, no magnificent call to action. Elwood had no paper, no pen, just walls, and he was all out of fine thoughts, let alone the wisdom and the way with words. The world had whispered its rules to him for his whole life and he refused to listen, hearing instead a higher order. The world continued to instruct: Do not love for they will disappear, do not trust for you will be betrayed, do not stand up for you will be swatted down. Still he heard those higher imperatives: Love and that love will be returned, trust in the righteous path and it will lead you to deliverance, fight and things will change. He never listened, never saw what was plainly in front of him, and now he had been plucked from the world altogether. The only voices were those of the boys below, the shouts and laughter and fearful cries, as if he floated in a bitter heaven.

A jail within a jail. In those long hours, he struggled over Reverend King's equation. *Throw us in jail and we will still love you . . . But be assured that we will wear you down by our capacity to suffer, and one day we will win our freedom.*

We will not only win freedom for ourselves, we will so appeal to your heart and your conscience that we will win you in the process and our victory will be a double victory. No, he could not make that leap to love. He understood neither the impulse of the proposition nor the will to execute it.

When he was little, he kept lookout on the dining room of the Richmond Hotel. It had been closed to his race and one day it would open. He waited and waited. In the dark cell, he reconsidered his vigil. The recognition he sought went beyond brown skin—he was looking for someone who looked like him, for someone to claim as kin. For others to claim him as kin, those who saw the same future approaching, slow as it may be and overfond of back roads and secret hardscrabble paths, attuned to the deeper music in the speeches and hand-painted signs of protest. Those ready to commit their weight to the great lever and move the world. They never appeared. In the dining room or anywhere else.

The door to the stairwell opened, scraping against the floor. Footsteps outside the dark cell. Elwood braced himself for another beating. After three weeks they had finally decided what to do with him. He was sure that was the only reason he hadn't been taken out back to the iron rings and then disappeared—uncertainty. Now that things had quieted down, Nickel returned to proper discipline and the customs that had been handed down from generation to generation.

The bolt slid. There was one slim silhouette in the doorway. Turner shushed him and helped Elwood to his feet.

"They're going to take you out back tomorrow," Turner whispered.

"Yeah," Elwood said. Like Turner was talking about someone else. He was dizzy.

"We got to get, man."

Elwood puzzled over the *we.* "Blakeley."

"That nigger's passed out, man. Shhh!" He handed Elwood his glasses and clothes and shoes. They came from Elwood's locker, the ones he wore on his first day of school. Turner was also dressed in regular clothes, black trousers and a dark blue work shirt. *We.*

The Cleveland boys had replaced the creaky floorboards for the inspection; they missed a few. Elwood tilted his head to listen for noise from the house father's quarters. The couch was near the door. Many a boy had made the journey up the steps to rouse him from that couch when he slept through reveille. Blakeley did not stir. Elwood was stiff from his confinement and from the two beatings. Turner let him lean on him. He carried a bulging knapsack on his back.

There was a chance they might happen on one of the boys from room 1 or room 2 heading out for a piss. They hurried, as quietly as they could, down and around the next flight of stairs. "We going to walk straight past," Turner said, and Elwood knew he meant past the rec room to the back entrance of Cleveland. The lights were on all night on the first floor. Elwood didn't know what time it was—one in the morning? two—but it was late enough for the night supervisors to be deep in some illicit shut-eye.

"They're playing poker down at the motor pool tonight," Turner said. "We'll see."

Once they got out of the light cast from the windows, they made a hobbled sprint for the main road. They were out.

Elwood didn't ask where they were headed. He asked Turner, "Why?"

"Shit—they were running around like bugs the last two

days, all those motherfuckers. Spencer. Hardee. Then Freddie told me that Sam heard from Lester that he heard them talking about taking you out back." Lester was a Cleveland kid who swept up at the supervisor's office and had the line on all the big stuff going down, a regular Walter Cronkite. "That was it," Turner said. "Tonight or not at all."

"But why are you coming with me?" He could have pointed Elwood in the right direction and wished him luck.

"They snatch you up in a hot minute, dumb as you are."

"You said don't take anyone with you," Elwood said. "On the run."

"You're dumb, and I'm stupid," Turner said.

Turner was taking him toward town, running along the road and then diving when a car appeared. As the houses got closer together, they crouched and took it slowly, which suited Elwood fine. His back hurt, and his legs where Spencer and Hennepin had sliced at him with Black Beauty. The immediacy of their flight reduced the pain. Three times somebody's damned dogs started up loud barking when they passed their houses and the boys sprinted. They never saw the dogs but the noise got their blood flowing.

"He's in Atlanta all month," Turner said. He'd led them to Mr. Charles Grayson's house, the banker they'd sung "Happy Birthday" to the night of the big fight. For Community Service they had cleaned out and painted his garage. It was a big house, and lonely. His twin sons had gone off to college. Elwood and Turner had thrown out a lot of the old toys from when the Grayson boys were little. They had matching red bicycles, Elwood remembered. The bikes were still where they'd left them, next to the gardening tools. The moonlight was enough to make them out.

Turner pumped up the tires. He didn't have to search for the pump. How long had he been planning this? Turner kept his own kind of records—this house provided one sort of aid, that house another—the same way Elwood maintained his.

There was no outfoxing the dogs once they were on the trail, Turner told him. "Most you can do is get as far away as you can. Put some miles between you and them." He tested the tires with his thumb and forefinger. "I think Tallahassee is good," he said. "It's big. I'd say north but I don't know up there. In Tallahassee we can get a ride somewhere and then those dogs going to need wings to catch us."

"They were going to kill me and bury me out there," Elwood said.

"Sure as shit."

"You got me out," Elwood said.

"Yup," Turner said. He started to say something else, but stopped. "Can you ride it?"

"I can do it."

It was an hour and a half to Tallahassee in a car. On a bike? Who knew how far they'd get before sunup, taking the roundabout way. The first time a car came up behind them and it was too late to veer off, they biked on and kept their faces blank. The red pickup overtook them without incident. After that, they remained on the road to make as many miles as Elwood's pace allowed.

The sun came up. Elwood was heading home. He knew he couldn't stay but it would calm him to be in his city again after these white streets. He'd go wherever Turner instructed and when it was safe, put it all down on paper again. Try the *Defender* again, and *The New York Times.*

They were the paper of record, which meant they were in the business of protecting the system, but they had come a long way in their coverage of the rights struggle. He could reach out to Mr. Hill again. Elwood hadn't tried to contact his former teacher after he got to Nickel—his lawyer had promised to track him down—but the man knew people. People in SNCC and those in the Reverend King's circle. Elwood had failed, but he had no choice but to take up the challenge again. If he wanted things to change, what else was there to do but stand up?

Turner, for his part, thought of the train they'd jump, he thought of the north. It wasn't as bad as down here—a Negro could make something of himself. Be his own man. Be his own boss. And if there was no train, he'd crawl on his hands and knees.

The morning got on and the traffic picked up. Turner had deliberated over this road or the other country road and picked this one. On the map it looked less populated and the same, distance-wise. He was sure the drivers were checking them out. Looking straight ahead was best. Elwood kept pace, to his surprise. Around the curve, the road lifted to a slope. If Turner had been locked up and had his ass kicked a few times, he'd be laid out going up this hill, little as it was. Sturdy—that was Elwood.

Turner drove his knee down with his hand. He'd stopped looking back when he heard a car behind them but he got a tingle and turned his head. It was a Nickel van. Then he saw the bloom of rust on the front fender. It was the Community Service van.

On one side of the road was farmland—dirt mounds in furrows—and on the other open pasture. No woods beyond them as far as he saw. The pasture was closer, surrounded by a white wooden fence. Turner shouted to his partner. They were going to have to run.

They steered to the bumpy side of the road and leapt off the bikes. Elwood made it over the fence before Turner did. One of the cuts on his back had bled through his shirt and dried. Turner caught up in a second and the boys were side by side. They ran through the tall swaying wild grass and weeds. The doors of the van opened and Harper and Hennepin climbed over the fence, quick. They each carried a shotgun.

Turner took a peek. "Faster!"

Down the slope lay another fence, and then trees.

"We got it!" Turner said.

Elwood panted, his mouth agape.

The first shotgun blast missed. Turner checked again. It was Hennepin. Harper stopped next. He held the shotgun like his daddy showed him when he was a boy. His daddy wasn't around much but had taught him this thing.

Turner zagged and put his head down as if he could duck buckshot. *Can't catch me, I'm the Gingerbread Man.* He looked back again as Harper pulled the trigger. Elwood's arms went wide, hands out, as if testing the solidity of the walls of a long corridor, one he had traveled through for a long time and which possessed no visible terminus. He stumbled forward two steps and fell into the grass. Turner kept running. He asked himself later if he heard Elwood cry out or make any kind of sound but never did figure it out. He was running and there was only the rush and roil of blood in his head.

EPILOGUE

Those kiosks didn't like him, no matter how much he jabbed and muttered at the screens. He checked in at the counter. This one's attendant was a black girl in her mid-twenties, all business. That new breed coming up, like Millie's nieces, who didn't take any mess and weren't afraid to tell you.

"Flying to Tallahassee," Turner said. "Last name Curtis."

"Identification?"

He was due for a new driver's license, now that he shaved his head every other day. He didn't resemble the picture. The old him. Once he got to Tallahassee he wouldn't need this license anyhow. It was history.

When the owner of the diner asked him his name, two weeks out of Nickel, he said, "Elwood Curtis." First thing that popped into his head. It felt right. He used the name from then on when anybody asked, to honor his friend.

To live for him.

Elwood's death made the papers. He was a local boy, you can't escape the long arm of the law, that bullshit. Turner's name in black-and-white newsprint as the other escapee, "a Negro youth." No description apart from that. Another black boy causing trouble, that's all you needed to know. Turner hid out in Jaimie's old stomping grounds—the railroad yards in All Saints. He risked one night at the depot and then hopped a freight north. Working here and there—restaurants, day labor, construction—up the coast. Eventually New York City, where he stayed.

In 1970, he went back to Florida for the first time and requested a copy of Elwood's birth certificate. The downside of working with sketchy dudes on building sites and in greasy spoons was that they were sketchy, but they also knew shady things, like how to get a birth certificate for a dead man. Dead boy. Date of birth, name of parents, city. Back then it was easy, before Florida wised up and put all those protections in place. He put in for a Social Security card two years later and it arrived in the mailbox, sitting on top of an A&P flyer.

The printer behind the airline counter chattered and whirred. "You have a good flight, sir," the attendant said. She smiled. "Anything else?"

He woke up. "Thank you." Lost in that old place. His first visit to Florida in forty-three years. The place reached right through the TV screen and yanked him back.

Millie got home from work last night and he gave her the two articles he printed out on Nickel and the graveyards. "That's terrible," she said. "These people get away with everything." According to one of the pieces, Spencer had died some years before, but Earl was still kicking around. Ninety-five years old, all of them wretched. He was retired, and such "a well-respected member of the Eleanor community" that in 2009 the town bestowed their Good Citizen of the Year Award on him. In the newspaper photo the old supervisor was decrepit, leaning on a cane on his porch, but his cold steel eyes gave Turner a shiver.

"Did you ever hit boys thirty or forty times with a strap?" the reporter asked.

"That is simply not true, sir. I swear on my children's lives. Just a little discipline," Earl said.

Millie gave him back the articles. "You know that old cracker beat them boys. *A little discipline.*"

She didn't get it. How could she, living in the free world her whole life. "I used to live there," Turner said.

His tone. "Elwood?" Like testing the ice to see if it'd bear her weight.

"I was at Nickel. That's the place. I told you I was in juvie, but I never said the name."

"Elwood. Come here," she said. He sat on the couch. He hadn't served his time, as he told her years ago, but ran. Then he told her the rest, including the story of his friend. "His name was Elwood," Turner said.

They were on the couch for two hours. Not counting the fifteen minutes, halfway through, that she spent in their bedroom with the door closed: "I have to go, I'm sorry." She returned, her eyes rubbed red, and they picked it up.

In some ways Turner had been telling Elwood's story ever since his friend died, through years and years of revisions, of getting it right, as he stopped being the desperate alley cat of his youth and turned into a man he thought Elwood would have been proud of. It was not enough to survive, you have to live—he heard Elwood's voice as he walked down Broadway in the sunlight or at the end of a long night hunched over the books. Turner walked into Nickel with strategies and hard-won dodges and a knack for keeping out of scrapes. He jumped over the fence on the other side of the pasture and into the woods and then both boys were gone. In Elwood's name, he tried to find another way. Now here he was. Where had it taken him?

Millie said, "Your falling out with Tom." Moments from nineteen years resolved into fine grain. It was easier to focus on details. Small things stuck and kept her from taking in the entire picture. His fight with Tom, who worked with him at his first moving job. They'd been friends a long time. It was a Fourth of July barbecue out in Port Jefferson, at the man's own house. They were talking about some rapper who just got out of jail for tax evasion and Tom said, "Don't do the crime, if you can't do the time," singing it like in the opening credits to that old cop show.

"That's why they get away with it," he said to Tom, "because people like you think they deserve it." Why was he—who? Elwood? Turner? the man she married—defending this deadbeat? Blowing up like that. Yelling at Tom in front of the whole party while he flipped burgers in that silly apron. They drove all the way back to Manhattan in silence. Other small things: Him walking out of movies with no explanation beyond "I'm bored" because a scene—of violence, of helplessness—abducted him and took him back to Nickel. He was always so calm and even then this darkness crept up on him. His rants about cops and the criminal justice system and predators—everyone hated cops, but it was different with him and she taught herself to let him vent when he got on one of his jags because of the feral thing that snuck into his face, the vehemence of his words. The nightmares that tormented him, the ones he claimed not to remember—she knew his reform school had been bad but she didn't know it had been this place. She took his head into her lap as he wept, running her thumb over that stray-cat notch in his ear. The scar she never noticed but was right in front of her.

Who was he? He was him, the man he had always been. She told him that she understood, as much as she was able to understand that first night. He was him. They were the same age. She had grown up in the same country with the same skin. She lived in New York City in 2014. It was hard to remember sometimes how bad it used to be—bending to a colored fountain when she visited her family in Virginia, the immense exertion white people put into grinding them down—and then it all returned in a rush, set off by tiny things, like standing on a corner trying to hail a cab, a routine humiliation she forgot five minutes later because if she didn't, she'd go crazy, and set off by the big things, a drive through a blighted neighborhood snuffed out by that same immense exertion, or another boy shot dead by a cop: They treat us like subhumans in our own country. Always have. Maybe always will. His name didn't matter. The lie was big but she understood it, given how the world had crumpled him up, the more she took in his story. To come out of that place and make something of himself, to become a man capable of loving her the way he did, to become the man she loved—his deception was nothing compared to what he had done with his life.

"I don't call my husband by his last name."

"Jack. Jack Turner." No one had ever called him Jack except his mother and his aunt.

"I'll try it on," she said. "Jack, Jack, Jack."

It sounded okay to him. More true each time it came out of her mouth.

They were wrung out. In their bed she said, "You have to tell me all of it. This isn't just one night."

"I know. I will."

"What if they throw you in jail?"

"I don't know what they're going to do."

She should go with him. She wanted to go with him. He wouldn't let her. They'd have to pick it up after he had done this thing. No matter which way it ended up down there.

They didn't speak after that. They didn't sleep. She curled into his spine, him reaching back for her rump to make sure she was still real.

The gate lady announced his Tallahassee flight. He had the row to himself. He stretched out and slept, he'd been up all night, and when he woke on the plane he picked up his argument with himself over betrayal. Millie had changed everything for him. Unbent him from who he had been. He betrayed her. And he had betrayed Elwood by handing over that letter. He should have burned it and talked him out of that fool plan instead of giving him silence. Silence was all the boy ever got. He says, "I'm going to take a stand," and the world remains silent. Elwood and his fine moral imperatives and his very fine ideas about the capacity of human beings to improve. About the capacity of the world to right itself. He had saved Elwood from those two iron rings out back, from the secret graveyard. They put him in Boot Hill instead.

He should have burned that letter.

From what he read in Nickel articles the last few years, they buried dead boys quick to head off any investigation, not even a word to their families—but then who had the money to bring them home and rebury them? Not Harriet. Turner found her obituary in the online archive of a Tallahassee paper. She died a year after Elwood, survived by her daughter, Evelyn. It didn't mention if the daughter had shown up for the funeral. Turner had the money now to bury his friend properly, but any redress was on hold. Like with what he'd say to Millie to show her who he was—he couldn't see anything past his return to Nickel.

In the taxi line outside the Tallahassee airport Turner wanted to bum a cigarette from the desperate smoker lighting up after being cooped up in the plane. Millie's stern face warned him off and he whistled "No Particular Place to Go" to distract himself. Once he was on the way to the Radisson, he checked the piece from the *Tampa Bay Times* again. He'd looked at it so often that his fingers smudged the printout—he had to complain to Yvette about the toner or whatnot when he got back, whenever that was. Ace Moving had a future, or it didn't.

The press conference was at eleven a.m. According to the paper, the sheriff of Eleanor was going to give an update on the investigation of the grave sites and an archaeology professor from the University of South Florida would speak on the forensic examinations of the dead boys. And some of the White House boys were going to be there to testify. He'd kept tabs on them through their website the last couple of years—the reunions, the stories of their life at the school and after, their attempts to be recognized. They wanted a memorial and an apology from the state. They wanted to be heard. He'd thought them pathetic, moaning about what happened forty, fifty years ago, but recognized now it was his own pitiable state that revolted him, how scared he got seeing the name of the place and the pictures. No matter the front he put up, nowadays and back then, his bravado in front of Elwood and other boys. He'd been scared all the time. He was scared still. The state of Florida closed the school three years ago and now it was all coming out, as if everyone, all the boys, had to wait for it to be dead before they told the tale. It couldn't hurt them now, snatch them up at midnight and brutalize them. It could only hurt them in the old familiar ways.

All the men on the website were white. Who spoke for the black boys? It was time someone did.

Seeing the grounds and the haunted buildings on the nightly news, he had to go back. To speak about Elwood's story, no matter what happened to him. Was he a wanted man? Turner didn't know the law but he had never underestimated the crookedness of the system. Not then, not now. What happens will happen. He'll find Elwood's grave and tell his friend of his life after he was cut down in that pasture. How that moment grew in Turner and changed his life's course. Tell the sheriff who he was, share Elwood's story and what they did to him when he tried to put a stop to their crimes.

Tell the White House boys that he was one of them, and he survived, like them. Tell anyone who cared that he used to live there.

The Radisson sat on a downtown corner of Monroe Street. It was an old hotel they'd added a bunch of floors to. The dark modern windows and brown metal siding of the new parts clashed with the red brick of the bottom three stories, but it was better than demolishing the place and starting anew. There was too much of that these days, especially in Harlem. All those buildings that had seen so much, and they go ahead and raze them. The old hotel made for a good foundation. It had been a long time since he'd seen that Southern architecture of his youth, with the open porches and white balconies running around the floors like ticker tape.

Turner checked into his room. His stomach growled after he opened his suitcase and he went back down to the hotel restaurant. It was an in-between time and the place was empty. The server slouched by the wait station, a pale teenage girl with dyed-black hair. She wore the T-shirt of a band he never heard of, black with a laughing green skull overlaid. Some heavy metal thing. She put down her magazine and said, "Sit anywhere you like."

The chain had redone the dining room in contemporary hotel style, with a lot of wipeable green plastic. Three tilted television sets nattered the same cable news station at different angles, the news was bad and ever was, and a pop song from the '80s blipped from hidden speakers, an instrumental version with the synthesizers out front. He looked the menu over and decided on a burger. The name of the restaurant—Blondie's!—poured forth on the front of the menu in puffy gold script, and below that was a brief paragraph on the history of the place. Formerly the Richmond Hotel, it was a Tallahassee landmark and great care, they said, had gone into preserving the spirit of the grand old establishment. The shop by reception sold postcards.

If he had been less tired he might have recognized the name from a story he heard once when he was young, about a boy who liked to read adventure stories in the kitchen, but it eluded him. He was hungry and they served all day, and that was enough.

ACKNOWLEDGMENTS

This book is fiction and all the characters are my own, but it was inspired by the story of the Dozier School for Boys in Marianna, Florida. I first heard of the place in the summer of 2014 and discovered Ben Montgomery's exhaustive reporting in the *Tampa Bay Times.* Check out the newspaper's archive for a firsthand look. Mr. Montgomery's articles led me to Dr. Erin Kimmerle and her archaeology students at the University of South Florida. Their forensic studies of the grave sites were invaluable and are collected in their *Report on the Investigation into the Deaths and Burials at the Former Arthur G. Dozier School for Boys in Marianna, Florida.* It is available at the university's website. When Elwood reads the school pamphlet in the infirmary, I quote from their report on the school's day-to-day functions.

Officialwhitehouseboys.org is the website of Dozier survivors, and you can go there for the stories of former students in their own words. I quote White House Boy Jack Townsley in chapter four, when Spencer is describing his attitude toward discipline. Roger Dean Kiser's memoir, *The White House Boys: An American Tragedy*, and Robin Gaby Fisher's *The Boys of the Dark: A Story of Betrayal and Redemption in the Deep South* (written with Michael O'McCarthy and Robert W. Straley) are excellent accounts.

Nathaniel Penn's *GQ* article "Buried Alive: Stories From Inside Solitary Confinement" contains an interview with an inmate named Danny Johnson in which he says, "The worst thing that's ever happened to me in solitary confinement happens to me every day. It's when I wake up." Mr. Johnson spent twenty-seven years in solitary confinement; I have recast that quote in chapter sixteen. Former prison warden Tom Murton wrote about the Arkansas prison system in his book with Joe Hyams called *Accomplices to the Crime: The Arkansas Prison Scandal.* It provides a ground's-eye view of prison corruption and was the basis of the movie *Brubaker,* which you should see if you haven't. Julianne Hare's *Historic Frenchtown: Heart and Heritage in Tallahassee* is a wonderful history of that African-American community over the years.

I quote the Reverend Martin Luther King Jr. a bunch; it was energizing to hear his voice in my head. Elwood cites his "Speech Before the Youth March for Integrated Schools" (1959); the 1962 LP *Martin Luther King at Zion Hill,* specifically the "Fun Town" section; his "Letter from Birmingham Jail"; and his 1962 speech at Cornell College. The "Negroes are Americans" James Baldwin quote is from "Many Thousands Gone" in *Notes of a Native Son.*

I was trying to see what was on TV on July 3, 1975. *The New York Times* archive has the TV listings for that night, and I found a good nugget.

This is my ninth book with Doubleday. Many, many thanks to Bill Thomas, my excellent and exalted editor and publisher, and to Michael Goldsmith, Todd Doughty, Suzanne Herz, Oliver Munday, and Margo Shickmanter for their abundant support, hard work, and faith over the years.

Thanks to Nicole Aragi, agent extraordinaire, without whom I am just another writer bum, and to Grace Dietsche and to all the Aragi crew. Thanks to the nice people at the Book Group for their encouraging words. And much gratitude and love to my family—Julie, Maddie, and Beckett. Lucky is the man to have these people in his life.

Also by Colson Whitehead

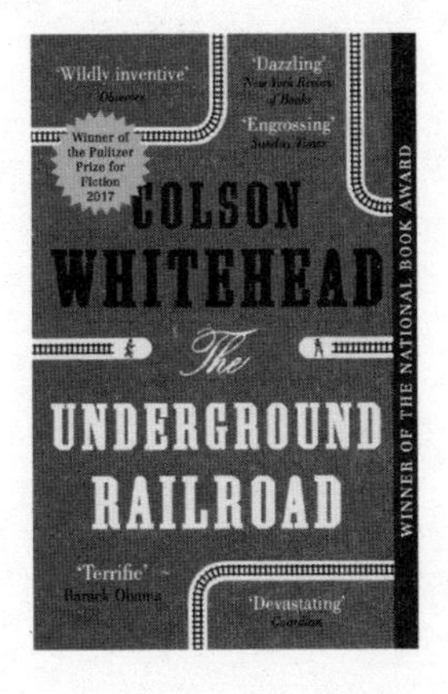

Cora is a slave on a cotton plantation in Georgia, an existence made even more hellish by her status as an outcast among her fellow Africans. And she is approaching womanhood, where greater pain and danger awaits. So when Caesar, a slave recently arrived from Virginia, tells her about the Underground Railroad, Cora takes the momentous decision to accompany him on his escape to the North.

In this razor-sharp novel, the Underground Railroad has assumed a physical form, a dilapidated box-car pulled by a steam locomotive, picking up fugitives wherever it can. Thus begins Cora's perilous journey, as she is pursued by a ruthless slave-catcher named Ridgeway, obsessed both with Cora and her mother, who eluded him years before.

The Underground Railroad is the story of one woman's ferocious will to escape the horrors of bondage, and a shatteringly powerful meditation on history and the unfulfilled promises of the present day.